LOVE
ME
DEADLY

Blossom Elfman

FAWCETT JUNIPER • NEW YORK

RLI: $\dfrac{\text{VL: 5 \& up}}{\text{IL: 6 \& up}}$

A Fawcett Juniper Book
Published by Ballantine Books
Copyright © 1989 by Blossom Elfman

All rights reserved under International and Pan-American Copyright Conventions. Published in the United States by Ballantine Books, a division of Random House, Inc., New York, and simultaneously in Canada by Random House of Canada Limited, Toronto.

Library of Congress Catalog Card Number: 88-92196

ISBN 0-449-70298-7

Manufactured in the United States of America

First Edition: April 1989

For Lola Elfman

With special thanks to Gavi Yariv

1

"Just tell me why?" asked Francine. "When you could have any guy in the school, why would you pick the only one who doesn't absolutely fall apart when you snap your fingers?"

I shushed her and shoved her back behind the lockers. He was coming down the corridor, his nose in a book, as usual. Of course Francine was right. I could have had anyone. I'm not bragging. It's just that I grew up here in Martindale. I've known all the guys since nursery school. And okay, I also happen to have good features, chestnut hair, and violet eyes.

"Violent" eyes, Arthur Sampson calls them. My trouble was that I didn't want Arthur Sampson or any of them, football team or not. I wanted the only guy nobody could get close to. Ask me why.

I can't tell you.

His name was Michael Sloane. He lived out in the country. He biked in. And after school he biked out. He'd been here at Martindale High since last term. He was in no sports, no clubs, nothing. He ate lunch with a book in front of his face. He was a genius, absolutely brilliant.

"What makes him so special?" Francine asked. I just didn't *know*. Okay, he happened to look like a young, blond Christopher Reeve: tall, broad in the shoulders, hair that fell over his brow and down the back of his neck, soft eyes that absolutely melted me down, even behind those Clark Kent glasses.

And he was straight A. I never heard a teacher ask him a question he couldn't answer. He'd take in the question, let it settle, pull on his left earlobe—always his left—and then he'd pour out an answer and leave us all with jaws unhinged.

Me, I'm lucky if I pull a low B. So I fall for the only boy in Martindale High who walks by me without even looking my way, as he was about to do now.

So I did something really wretched. I stepped out into his path. He was so absorbed, he didn't even notice until we collided. "Oh!" I said. "I'm so sorry! I wasn't looking where I was going!"

And I'm smiling, I mean my best smile, the one that makes my nose wrinkle, that adorable smile, at least that's what Richard Cooper said after the junior class dance last Saturday night. So I waited. He looked at me as if I were a stone in his path, or some weird impediment to his smooth journey, and without a word or a nod or anything, he turned back to his book and walked on. Francine put her arm around me. "Happens to me all the time. Honestly, is he worth it?"

I wanted to say no! But my heart wouldn't let me. Something about him kept making me write Mike and Ally over the front of my notebook.

So Francine and I trudged into town and found an empty

table at Bozo's and ordered banana splits. Francine looked down at the three scoops, the hot fudge, the bananas, the cherry, the nuts, and the whipped cream. "This is going to kill me," she moaned. "I'm the only sixteen-year-old I know who already has cellulite on her thighs. I'm going on this super new diet starting Monday. Complex carbohydrate. You can eat all the spaghetti you want."

I drowned my disappointment in hot fudge and whipped cream. I never put on an ounce because I ran it off. Five miles every morning. I'm a good runner, and if anyone says that I'm running after Michael Sloane, they'd better watch out. I'm also a kick boxer. My father feels that a girl has to protect herself. I also swim, ski, and sometimes I hang glide with my father when he's between flights. He's a pilot for T.W.A. For a while I went skydiving. Until my mother found out and marched into my room, fire in her eyes, and announced in that *voice*, "Allison McNeil, you are grounded for a month!"

Okay. I'm not perfect. Sometimes I use bad judgment. I'm just telling you this so you'll understand that jumping out of planes and floating through open space don't bother me.

A guy who walks by me as if I'm air, that bothers me.

I was brooding about all of that with my spoon scraping the last of the fudge and swirling it with the last of the whipped cream when Arnie came running in. Arnie Halperin, who is about five feet tall and plays the electric guitar, very badly. He dropped himself in the chair in total disgust. "I asked myself," he said, wolfing down Francine's chocolate chip cookie which came with the banana split and which she was guarding jealously, "I asked myself, how could the faculty of Martindale High be worse? I mean, the school was built right after the Flood, right? The faculty has been here since World War I. Mr. Evanston, the principal, keeps forgetting his lines at graduation, he's so old. Mrs. Bilger in Home Ec dropped her partial bridge in the creamed chipped beef. I mean, everyone knows that most of them are ready to retire except Bragg, and he's a total bastard. So guess what?"

"I'll kill you for eating that cookie," said Francine. "It was my last cookie before my complex carbohydrate diet."

Arnie leaned across the table and reached for my cookie, but I gave him a chop to the fingers. Hard. He put his hand under his armpit. "So you heard that Mr. Nightengale left for Florida. The VP slot is open. Now all they have to do is go into Olympia or Seattle or somewhere and get a real live teacher. Do you know who at this moment is moving into the VP's office?"

Francine looked at my cookie. "Are you absolutely going to eat it?"

"Bragg is getting the job."

Now both of us woke out of our banana-split dream. "Bragg? I thought somebody was going to get him fired!" I sputtered. "Do you know what he did when Michael Pullan talked during a geometry test? He drew a circle on the blackboard and made him stand with his nose in it for half an hour. He's a sadist!"

"He's also the new VP, which means he's heading up the prom committee, the sports committee."

It was totally depressing.

To make it worse, I had an appointment with the VP the next morning for cutting a particular class. It wasn't actually a cut. There happened to be a skydive meet up near Anacortes, and since I wasn't allowed to *do* it, my father said he'd take me to watch it. I had this note to give to the office, and I happened to lose it. What was I going to do? I wrote one myself and signed it. I know it was wrong. I'm not excusing myself. I told you, I'm not perfect. The only one who is perfect is Michael Sloane. At least I pictured him that way.

I did not sleep well that night. Even with Ruggles, my favorite old bear dragged out of the old toy trunk, to comfort me.

I sludged into the office the next morning to submit to the full extent of the law. Mr. Nightengale's law had never been much. He'd look at you with his watery eyes, take off his always-smudged glasses, and sigh and recite you a line out of Ovid or somebody Greek that in translation was supposed to make you feel guilty for transgressing the law. But Bragg! Whose name was even now being painted on the pebbled glass window! I was in deep dark trouble.

I was sitting on the "mourners' bench," as it was lovingly called, waiting to hear my name. Miss Finister, the school secretary, was sorting out stacks of paper, glowering at me. Miss Finister glowered at everyone. Miss Finister owned the school. Everyone knew that. She kept all the supplies locked in the storeroom, and she had the only key. If anyone wanted supplies when she was absent, too bad. Even the principal was afraid of her. She had a voice like a razor and a temper like a pit bull. I tried to make myself invisible.

Red Arnold, the maintenance man, came in for something. He started to ask, saw that it was Miss Finister and not her really sweet mousy little assistant, and did an about-face to get out of there. "Mr. Arnold," ground Miss Finister's saw-toothed voice. Red Arnold was an ex-rodeo rider. He was built like a good ol' boy, small in the hips and belly. I guess he used to drink more than beer because he had a big bulbous nose. But he was really nice. He'd tell us stories about roping and the old rodeo days. He was in A.A. He always said right out: "Kids, don't ever get hooked on the booze. It will finish you. It almost finished me. I was only saved by the A.A." He was one of the best. And he was not happy about Miss Finister's absolutely frigid glance. "Mr. Arnold. I looked over the time card.

You're punched in for three hours during which I happen to know you weren't on the job."

His face turned beet red. He looked at me helplessly. He swallowed hard. "That was only to fill in for three hours when I forgot to punch in. I never lied about my hours."

"Never? You did this time. I'm going to see to it that you're terminated. So get your things together."

He was an old cowboy. His eyes were full of the open range and John Wayne and all that. "You can't do this to me. You know that I need the job. I love this school, I love the kids—"

"If you loved it so much, you should have been more careful."

She'd already turned away coldly. He took off his hat—he always wore an ancient battered cowboy hat, the one he wore on the day he won the big rodeo prize up in Sooke, he'd told us that story a dozen times. He crumpled the hat between his big hams of hands, clenched his jaw. "You'll be sorry for this, you old hag."

I didn't smile. She *was* an old hag. But I felt too unhappy for him to enjoy hearing him say it.

And unhappy for me. I slouched down in my chair and waited for Bragg to call my name.

Garth Meacham walked in. Garth wore lots of leather and chains, he had his hair in some crazy punk style, and he drove a dirt bike. We always made it a point to keep a safe distance from Garth and his bunch. Now he stood in the office looking at Bragg's closed door with the same kind of dread I felt. Maybe he wasn't all that tough. He hiked up his shoulders, smoothed back his spiky hair, and walked to the counter. Miss Finister was counting pencils. "What is it?"

He cleared his throat. He always used this rough tough voice when he talked with the other guys. Now his voice was a little humbled. "Mr. Nightengale, he had me in yesterday. . . ."

"I know he had you in. You're suspended. What are you doing here?"

· If Red Arnold turned beet red, Garth turned a shade of off-gray. I could see he was affected. "No. He said he was going to give me another chance. We talked it over. He said he was giving me a pass to get back to class."

Miss Finister had eyes like black agates, cold and hard. "That was yesterday. You're a hoodlum. And Mr. Nightengale isn't here today, is he? I explained to Mr. Bragg what the situation was, and you're suspended. Now go home."

He planted his hands on the counter. "You don't know what you're doing. My old man, he'll—"

"Whatever he'll do, I'm sure you'll deserve it."

He was breathing hard. Poor Garth. I didn't have too much sympathy for a guy who roared around on his bike on Saturday nights when the rest of us were trying to talk or dance to somebody's radio in the square. He and his bunch were noise-makers, out for attention. But from the look on his face now, I guess he was in for it. His father drove a big rig truck and swaggered around like Arnold Schwarzenegger, looking for fights. And he knocked Garth around. We all knew that. Garth's eyes got teary. And then he saw me watching. He got out of there fast.

I was so miserable. I was up next. I only wanted to be out of that room, off running or something to get rid of that bad feeling. Mr. Bragg's door opened. *I* was in for it now.

Only he didn't look at me, not at first. Mr. Bragg was a rather slimy creature, very thin in the shoulders, a little thicker in the hips. His hair was receding, and his lips were pursy. He was the kind of guy who would make a poor helpless kid stick his nose to the circle on the blackboard and then make himself absolutely saccharine sweet to anyone who was above him or could do him favors. And if you wanted to make it up the ladder at Martindale High, you made yourself sweet to Miss Finister, which wasn't easy. "Margaret," he said, as if butter would melt in his mouth. (I didn't know her name was Margaret. It was hard for me to accept that anyone as sour as she was could have a nice first name.) "Margaret, I'll need a new blotter for my office desk." He smiled. The crown on one of his upper molars gleamed. "New broom, so to speak."

She didn't stop counting her pencils. She left him hanging there.

He cleared his throat. I could see by his eyes that he was puzzled by her attitude, and then the puzzlement went to a kind of discomfort. He smiled again. "I asked if I could have a new desk set out of the supply room."

She set her pencils down. "You won't need it."

He absolutely froze. I mean, he went rigid for a moment. And then this little sliver of a twitch went down his cheek. "What are you talking about?"

She brushed back a few iron-gray strands of hair and caught them in the comb she used to keep her twist of a braid in place. "It happened to be a lovely morning. I took an early walk down by the river."

She said no more. She didn't need to. He looked as if he'd been slapped. He walked back into his office and slammed the door. I thought: What on earth would old Bragg be doing down by the river? Could he have been with a girl or something? Was that it? But what woman would sink so low as to go down to the river with slimy Bragg?

Nobody was going to want to see me that morning. And I was saved by the first-period bell. I literally ran to class. English. Francine had been waiting for me outside the office. She had to run to keep up. "So what happened?"

"Plenty. See you during the break. Have I got things to tell you."

I hurried down the aisle of American lit and slid into my seat. I had been so worried this morning, I hadn't prepared my *Moby Dick*. Mr. Emerson taught American lit. He was the best teacher in the whole school. Everyone loved him. He looked like a Santa Claus, with a paunch of a belly and white wispy brows that touched when he wrinkled his forehead in some mock concern. He read aloud to us with great passion. I adored him. So did Michael Sloane, who sat about three seats up. Mr. Emerson was everyone's favorite. He was the only teacher in Martindale High who actually liked Miss Finister. In fact, they sometimes ate lunch together, which shows you how wonderful and tolerant he was.

Mr. Emerson moved to the front of the room, took a precarious seat on the edge of his solid desk. "And so, Allison . . ."

Me. I tried to sink deep into my chair.

"Explain to us how Herman Melville happened to call his white whale *Moby* Dick."

My father always said, Ally, when you don't know the answer, be smart enough to keep your mouth shut. The trouble with me was that I always had to have the last word. But I didn't have a word to answer. So I took a wild shot. "Well, the whale was on the move and Captain Ahab couldn't catch him, so maybe he called him 'mobile' Dick and then just shortened it down?" I said it as a question, like floating bait on a hook and then hoping.

Nobody laughed because nobody actually knew the answer, and I might just have been right.

Mr. Emerson smiled and stroked the side of his nose, the way Santa Claus did in all the kids' story books. "Mike?" he asked. Mike. I loved that name. I wrote it on my notebook cover. Again.

Mike took off his glasses and cleaned them on the edge of his sweater. "Actually the whale wasn't really white, it

was a light-colored whale, and he called it *Mocha* Dick.
And somehow in the editing, it got changed to Moby,
which evidently sounded better."

About thirty pairs of eyes looked to Emerson for confir-
mation. They couldn't believe that answer. It sounded too
dumb. "Exactly right," said Mr. Emerson.

There was a great gasp of amazement.

Also a look from me. Not only amazement. I was utterly mad to have a thing for this absolute computer-brain
of a guy. Anyhow, how did I know what his life was like
on the outside? Maybe he had a girl somewhere, some
really brilliant person like himself. Mr. Emerson opened
his book, and had just begun to read when an office worker
came in with a note. Mr. Emerson glanced at it, excused
himself, told us to read on, he'd be back in five minutes. I
sank into my book the way the harpoons sank into the cold
icy water of the whale-swum sea.

I didn't notice him coming back into the room. He
shocked everyone awake when he began to read. About
baby whales being born underwater and how the umbilical
cords got tangled in the harpoon lines. It was so awful. He
was shaken by what he read, you could tell that.

I was jolted out of *Moby Dick* by shouting voices. Outside. Something was going on. All of us turned and rub-
bernecked toward the window. A policeman was running
across the quad. And then another. Now everyone ran to
the window to see what was going on. We could hear
sirens. The ambulance pulled up right on campus, between
us and the office.

The second-period bell rang.

I ran along with everyone else to see what had happened. There was a crowd outside of the office. Aside
from Chief Mitchell, there are only five policemen on the
whole Martindale force, and they were all there, ordering
kids to stand back. I tried to get a glimpse of what was

going on. I happen to be very inquisitive. My mother has always said that it's one of my least attractive points. I can never keep my nose out of things. I just happen to be curious. And nobody was paying any attention to the side door. I always used the side door last year when I had messages to deliver during office practice. So I just slipped inside. There was such a crush in there, nobody noticed me. I saw that the storeroom door was open. Through the open door I could see that somebody had vandalized the supply cupboard. Books everywhere, ink thrown around, typewriters overturned on the floor. What on earth! There was a photographer snapping pictures. Not of the mess in the supply room, but of *shoes* that stuck out from under the supply table. Two shoes. Two sensible black shoes with low sensible heels. Miss Finister wore shoes like those!

Before one of the policemen managed to edge me out of the door, I saw something that shocked me totally. Miss Finister was still in those shoes! And judging from the white sheet that covered her, Miss Finister was dead!

2

"Murder!" My mother was absolutely horrified. "Here? In Martindale? Perhaps in Seattle or even in Olympia, but not in Martindale! And who on earth would want to kill Miss Finister?"

"Everyone!" our voices echoed, Francine's, Arnie's, and mine. The horrible murder of Miss Finister was all that anyone talked about. And not only in Martindale but in Paris, where my father was on a two-day layover. Long distance, I heard his shocked voice: "Not in Martindale!"

My father loved what he called the great Northwest. He'd traveled the whole world; so had my mother when she worked as a flight attendant. We lived just miles from the rocky Northwest Coast, a skip away from the mountains with its wild and unpredictable St. Helens, near the wonderful placid islands of Puget Sound, a half day's leisurely trip from Canada. To my father, this was paradise!

Well, I guess it was, if you look at it that way. But there

were no rock concerts in Martindale. You had to go up to Seattle. There was one movie theater, and Mr. Evanston had a great deal of influence on the city council and therefore on Mrs. Vilners who ran the Roxie, so we had a mess of Walt Disney, and no violence, which to Mrs. Vilners meant no raised voices and no bad language. Using "who" for "whom" was bad language to Mr. Evanston, which about eliminated every good movie anyone wanted to see. If it weren't for home video, we would have lived in the nineteenth century.

So our idea of a big Saturday night was sitting in front of the TV with popcorn and root beer, watching *The Fly*. Now, *The Fly* is supposed to be a scary movie. This humongous half-insect creature comes lunging at you. You're supposed to scream with fright, right? On a stupid nineteen-inch screen in your own living room, you feel like swatting it. So it was either that, or we got together in the town square and danced to somebody's portable radio. Or we went to Bozo's for ice cream. It's called Bozo's because they ran a lot of children's parties there. Outside was this huge statue of a clown with a big red nose. You ate your ice cream and felt about three years old. The only other social place was "down by the river" where at least you had silence and soft banks and the sound of water running over rocks. So that was Martindale: a Big Buy Supermarket, a McDonald's, a Pizza Time We Deliver, a few good stores (one of them was my mother's dress boutique). For more than that you went into Olympia or made a day of it and went into Seattle.

Now suddenly our quiet little town was the subject of talk in a Paris bistro where pilots had gathered. "You girls watch yourself!" my father warned. And he asked to talk to my brother, Orville.

Orville is twelve, short, and a real misery. Well, you couldn't blame him for being less than pleasant with a name like that. My father happened to fall in love with flying at the age of one, and Orville Wright was his hero. Orville had tried to change that name ever since he could talk. What can you do with Orville? Orrie? Villie? Orvie? So I gave him the only natural name under the circumstances: *Awful.*

Which he was. Sneak and snitch, a real little gameplayer. He took the phone. I could see him trying to stand tall to talk to my father in Paris. My father is six four, and Orville prays at night to grow tall. I've heard him through the wall. Really gross. In a world full of hunger and war and nuclear terror that he should actually try to bother God to make him tall. Anyhow, Orville got on the phone, trying to look really important, listening to his father on a terribly expensive overseas call telling him to protect the family. Ludicrous. When there's a storm, one crack of lightning, he's in my bed with his head under the covers. He hung up and said: "Don't worry, I'll keep an eye on the house while Dad's gone."

Good luck. "So what do you think?" Francine asked. "Who did it? Garth or Bragg or Mr. Arnold?"

"I vote for Garth," Arnie said. "He's really vicious."

"I'm not sure," I said. "I vote for Mr. Bragg. What do you suppose went on down by the river? Miss Finister has a lot of clout with Mr. Evanston. If she had something juicy to tell, she definitely could have ruined the new job for Mr. Bragg."

My mother came into the room with her new pattern and her pincushion. "Now I want the three of you to stay out of this. This is a matter for the police."

Arnie was beginning to get nervous. "I just thought— Ally is probably the last person to see old Finister alive. And the only one who knows that three people had it in for her."

Francine got owl-eyed. "He's right. Maybe they're all

just beginning to realize that you just might tell the police."

Orville was hopping up and down—he has this habit when he needs to say something and can't break into the conversation. He stalks, waving his arms, moving here and there to find a physical opening, and finally he blurts something out, the way he did now. "Maybe they're watching the house right now, trying to find a way to rub you out!"

My mother was crouched back on her heels, adjusting a hemline on a really adorable little summer dress she was designing for the shop. She fell back on her rear, sat there terribly alarmed. "Don't even say that as a joke! First thing in the morning, you go to Captain Mitchell and tell him what you know! I can't believe that this is happening in Martindale."

"I can't believe all of you are talking like this," I said. "Look. They said she was strangled. And they said there was no rope or marks of a rope. So somebody must have choked her. There must be fingerprints all over the place. They'll know who did it."

"Strangled her with bare hands," Francine said. "Then it had to be Red Arnold. He used to rope steers. He has hands like hams."

"So has Garth," Arnie said. "He works out at the gym on weekends. He's got hands like steel. I can prove it. Once when he was about twelve, he arm-wrestled me to the ground. He's vicious, I mean it."

No. That didn't feel right. "I remember seeing Garth that afternoon, after it happened. If he'd done it, he would have run, wouldn't he?"

My mother put in the last pin, made some notes on her pattern, and went to get dinner. She outdid herself with lasagna, the one with three cheeses, a Caesar salad with fried croutons, and her Chocolate Sin cake, which is so rich Rockefeller should have had it on his family crest.

I wasn't hungry. I was really worried. It was true. I was probably the only one to see the triple threat against Miss Finister. And it was odd, I thought as I fiddled with the lasagna, that Mr. Bragg hadn't told the police about my being in the office. Or they would have called me in, wouldn't they? And Garth, well, I saw him in the cafeteria that afternoon, sitting alone over a cup of cocoa, staring into the cup. Now that I thought about it, I remember that Garth looked up from his cup and caught my eye. It wasn't like a warning or anything, just a sort of curiosity. As if he were trying to figure me out.

"Is lasagna complex carbohydrate?" Francine asked. She was halfway through her second helping. She must have remembered her diet.

"Pasta is carbohydrate," my mother said, "but the cheese—"

"I'll just push off the cheese," Francine said, making a little move with her fork that eliminated about one square millimeter of mozzarella. And sprinkling the rest with Parmesan. The Chocolate Sin was brought in, a terrible temptation. Arnie needed calories. He took a double portion. My mind was working, and my nervous system was alerted. I wasn't hungry. Francine always eats when she's nervous. "This cake," she said, "must be very complex, and full of sugar. So I see it this way. I eat the cake, my body really goes to work hard to burn the calories. Then while it's still overworking, I start the diet. Tomorrow I really ought to lose something. What do you think?"

I thought that maybe I was really in trouble.

I had nightmares all night. Everyone was still asleep when I left for my before-school run. Usually I met other runners, or people stepping out onto their porches to bring in the Martindale *News Courier*. This morning I was utterly alone! I saw a few shades lifted, faces looking out. Something in Martindale had definitely changed, even in me as I ran through the park, down through the thicket that led to the river. I found myself listening for footsteps following me. It was only just beginning to strike me that there might be a murderer in town.

By the time I dressed for school, my mother and Orville were bent over the paper. "Captain Mitchell said there were definitely fingerprints," my mother said. Captain Mitchell was Mayor Wright's brother-in-law, a pretty clunky sort of man for a police captain. "He said he can't announce whose until the suspect is picked up. What suspect would stay around to be caught if he left fingerprints? He must have left town, so I suppose at least we're safe."

There was no use trying to see Mr. Bragg that morning because the office was closed off with yellow tape barriers that the police had set up. And if it *had* been Bragg, he was probably already across the Canadian border. I was swamped in my thoughts when I walked into American lit. Everyone was quietly whispering except Mike Sloane, who sat silently bent over his *Moby Dick*. Mike was not on my mind this morning. Garth and Red Arnold were.

It was only when Mr. Emerson walked into the room that we all realized what we should have remembered. He looked absolutely terrible: his tie badly done, a jacket that didn't match his pants, his hair mussed, and his eyes red-rimmed. Of course. He knew and liked Miss Finister! Now I saw Mike sit up, too, taking this in. Poor Mr. Emerson.

You only had to see the way he stumbled toward his desk, his eyes so distant and bereft. He reached into his jacket pocket and took out an old dog-eared leather-bound book. His hands trembled as he opened it and searched through pages. I'd never seen him like this. We all leaned forward. This time he didn't read in his marvelous deep sonorous tones, but softly, his voice cracking:

What lips my lips have kissed
And where and why I have forgotten . . .

It was a poem he'd read before. I'm not a poem person, but this one really touched me. About a lover who stands at the window and watches a lonely tree and knows that his only love will never return:

. . . I cannot say what loves have come and gone—

His voice broke. I could see tears in his eyes.

I only know that summer sang in me
A little while, that in me sings no more.

I was shocked to the center of my heart. Love? Did he mean *love*? Not for Miss Finister! I saw Mike Sloane lean forward, as if he were trying to see something in Mr. Emerson he hadn't seen before.

We were all caught in that moment of agonizing bewilderment when the door opened and two policemen walked in: Charlie Foresman, who sometimes works nights at the Big Buy Supermarket, and Marvin Letterman, who only joined on a year ago and goes up to Seattle two afternoons a week to finish his law degree. Marvin planted himself in front of the kindly, gentle Mr. Emerson and said: "Sir, do you mind stepping outside for a moment?"

Mr. Emerson got up slowly. He shuffled toward the door. The two policemen walked just behind him. An ominous hush fell over the classroom, and all ears and eyes devoured the scene going on just outside the open door.

Marvin Letterman squirmed. "Well, old man," he said, "I guess you know why we're here. Your fingerprints are all over the place. I arrest you for the murder of Margaret

Finister. And I have to tell you that anything you say now may be used against you."

Mr. Emerson dropped his head forward, tears running down his cheeks. They handcuffed him, an awful thing to do. He was about sixty. He couldn't have run if he wanted to. They led him away.

It wasn't my voice that broke out of shock first. It was Mike Sloane's. "No!" he bellowed. "It's not possible!"

My voice followed. "No! He couldn't have done it!"

I wanted to say more to Mike, but he'd already gathered up his books and rushed out of the room.

3

I caught up with him at the apple machine. He was standing against it, breathing hard, trying to regain his cool. "He didn't do it. I'd stake my life on it. I know him. He's a friend of mine."

"He's a friend of mine, too! And I know he didn't do it. He was the only one who liked Miss Finister. And I happen to know a few things nobody else does. There were others who had plenty of reason to hate her."

"Well, I happen to know a few things, too," Mike said, his eyes filled with total fury. "Tell me what it is you think you know, and I'll find out who really did it, I swear I will."

"Look," I said, "let's pool our information. Maybe we can work out what really happened."

"Pool what? This isn't a Saturday dance or a basketball game! This is his life and death! I don't need some featherhead girl to pool information with. Now just tell me what you know and let me go to work on it!"

I began to know how St. Helens felt before it started to blow steam and lava. *Feather*head?

Mike backed off an inch. "Well, I didn't mean it quite that way."

"No? Exactly how did you mean it?"

He took off his glasses and cleaned them on his shirt. "I'm sorry. I didn't mean to . . . look, I don't have time for apologies. We both know where you stand."

I had crossed my arms. I stood there rigidly. "And exactly where do I stand?"

"In the square on Saturday night drinking a Coke and dancing. And the rest of the time, who knows? You're never prepared in class, you don't give a darn about your schoolwork. I suppose all you really care about is guys and clothes."

"Clothes? What clothes!"

He put the glasses back on, but evidently they were still smudged, because he took them off again. "I see you almost every afternoon when I bike through town. In that dress shop trying on clothes. Let's face it. You're a silly kid. And a man's life is in danger. Now will you please tell me what it is you think you know?"

It was the clothes that got to me. Yes, I suppose I did like going into the square and having a Coke and dancing. I suppose he could think that was all I ever did. But I never bought clothes at all. My mother designed all my clothes. "My mother happens to own that dress shop! I happen to work with her every chance I get! And I try on the clothes because I'm her model. She patterns them on me! Featherhead? That's what I am? And what about you? You've been going to Martindale High for six months. Who knows you? You keep to yourself, you're so superior, you don't care about the school, you never support the games or anything. And after school you high-tail it home. Your whole life comes out of a book. So you're brilliant. Great! But you don't care about people."

I was beginning to lose steam. I was beginning to get teary, and I was absolutely positively not going to let him see me cry. "Share what I know with you? Not on your life. I'll show you who's a featherhead. I'll find out who killed Miss Finister and save Mr. Emerson if it's the last thing I do!"

I turned and walked away.

He could go take himself a running jump. I had been so wrong about him. I had totally misjudged him. He was insensitive and cruel and . . . and I never wanted to see him again. I heard someone walking after me. I picked up speed. Then I ran. I'm a very fast runner. I was home and up the stairs and in my room with the door closed. I was on my bed, curled into my pillow. Featherhead? Is that what I was? Maybe he was right. I pulled the covers over my head and cried.

Somebody pulled the covers off. Orville, with a peanut butter and jelly sandwich in his hand, sat on the edge of my bed. "What's the matter with you?"

I pulled the covers back. "Will you just get out of here and leave me alone?"

He pulled them off again. "So what's the matter? Dad said I was to take care of the girls until he got back. Did somebody hurt you or what?" Now I saw that in his other hand he had a baseball bat. He had been ordered to guard the women of the family. Poor frightened little kid, I knew him, I knew how he kept his hands in front of his face when we watched scary parts of *The Fly*.

"I guess someone did. It's not what you think. Somebody insulted me."

He pulled himself up to his full four feet something and

stuffed the rest of the sandwich into his mouth. The edges were all strawberry jelly. He wiped the sticky hand on my quilt. "Just tell me who it was. What did he do! I'll make him sorry that he ever insulted my sister."

Tears burst out fresh. "He said I was a silly airhead girl."

Orville lowered the bat. "Oh, is that all? That's not an insult, it's a fairly accurate description."

I threw my clock at him.

I sat glumly at dinner. My mother was on the phone with T.W.A. She hadn't heard from Daddy, and she was worried. There had been a storm in Europe somewhere and there was a flight delay. They were sure she'd hear from him soon. I fiddled with my food. "Honey," she said, "I know you must be upset about Mr. Emerson. What a nice old man. I can't believe he could have done such a terrible thing."

"He didn't," I said. "I'm really nervous. I have to take a run."

"Allison, it's too late to go running."

I slammed the door behind me. Mike Sloane lived out in the country near Puddleston. I had accidentally seen his records when I had office practice. Well, not exactly accidentally. I searched the files to find them. Puddleston was six miles, too far to run. I took my bike. I biked onto the highway. It was getting fairly dark. I wasn't exactly certain where near Puddleston, but I knew that I couldn't think of myself now, or my feelings. Mike Sloane knew something about Mr. Emerson. I had made myself a vow to find out the truth about Miss Finister and save Mr. Emerson and whether it cost me my pride or not, I was going to do it.

I stopped at a little Puddleston grocery. The man was just getting ready to lock up. "Can you tell me, please, do the Sloanes live anywhere near here?"

"First turn to the right, down the road, little farmhouse

end of the lane, behind the stand of rhododendrons."

Now that I was there, what was I supposed to say? I walked my bike up the path. I saw the house. It was a balmy night for Washington this time of the year. I saw a lantern on the porch of the old farmhouse, insects buzzing around it. There were two people sitting on the porch in the almost dark. One of them was Mike. He was bending close to someone, talking in low tones. No, not talking, he was reciting poetry. I recognized the lines. "... summer only sang in me a little while..." The lines Mr. Emerson had recited before they arrested him. Reading poetry to whom? I saw somebody wearing a shawl against the cool evening, somebody with longish hair. He had a girl, then. Out here. And he was reading her poetry.

I stepped on a dry stick. It cracked under my shoe. The two figures sat up straight, listening. I went hot with embarrassment. What was I going to say? Mike stood up. The light was fading. He saw me. Now I realized that the other figure wasn't a girl at all. It was a man, an old man, frail, long hair, a shawl about his shoulders. "Is that a visitor?" the old man asked.

I was stuck. How exactly was I going to explain why I was walking up a private road at this time of night? Mike said nothing. The old man had waved him back and leaned toward me, listening. I walked up the path, on the crunch of leaves. Crack, I hit my head. There was a low-hanging branch sticking out from the tree that grew in front of the porch. "Don't tell me," the old man said. I could see the bush of white hair now and the frail arms and the slender fingers of the hand as he seemed to brush the air with it. I could also see his eyes now. They were not focused on me. *The old man was blind!* "It's a girl, I think, from the sound of the weight on the leaves. Is that right, Mike? By the crunch of the leaves, I'd say about a hundred and twenty pounds, something like that. And tall, to hit your head on that branch you'd have to be, say, five foot seven. And so silent. A girl, perhaps a girl you've had some problem with, hey, Mike? Am I right?"

Mike put down his book. "Right again, Grandpa. This is Allison. Ally this is my grandfather, Mr. Sloane."

"Nice to meet you," I said, shaking the hand the old man extended as he rose.

"You, too, Ally," Mr. Sloane said, then added, "I judge you two have something to work out, so I'll leave you alone."

Feeling his way, he walked into the house. The screen door squeaked its slow closure and clicked shut.

I sat down at the edge of the step. I was dying of embarrassment. "Look, I didn't mean—"

"Neither did I." He came to sit beside me. "I didn't mean to hurt your feelings today. I guess I wasn't as observant as I thought. But I'm worried about Mr. Emerson."

"So am I. Look. Maybe I am a featherhead. But I'm a curious featherhead. And I know a few things. So let's make a truce. I tell you what I know, you tell me what you know. Is it a deal?"

"Deal. But once we do, it's understood that you stay out of it. If Mr. Emerson didn't kill Miss Finister, somebody else did, and I don't want to take the chance of anybody else getting hurt."

"No. That's the whole point! I want to be in it! I'm suggesting we work together."

He shook his head. "Absolutely not."

I stood up. "It's no use, is it? You're just pig-headed stubborn." I ran for my bike and started down the path toward the road. I heard him call after me. "Allison!" At least he knew my name.

Forget it.

I'd find a way to solve this mystery myself.

I pumped up the incline toward the Martindale road. It

was very dark now. I had to make plans. There were three possible suspects: Garth, Red Arnold, and slimy Bragg. Any one of them could have killed Miss Finister. And most important, I couldn't understand why Mr. Emerson didn't protest that he wasn't guilty when they arrested him. Why did he let them lead him away like that, like a sheep to slaughter?

I heard the roar of motors coming from town, a lot of them. Bikers. The only bike gang was Garth's. The Black Devils, they called themselves, with jackets they decorated with marking pens and tattoos they drew on themselves. I moved far to the side of the road. The gang passed me by, with a few hoots and a few comments. Gone. I felt a real sense of relief. Too soon. Now I heard one bike sputter, turn around, and come up behind me. My throat felt dry, not just from the incline.

Garth swung his wild-painted cycle in front of me. I jolted to a stop. My bike toppled over, and so did I. I scampered to my feet. "What—what do you want? I've got to get home. They're expecting me. My mom will probably be out with the car looking for me."

He sat on the cycle, balancing himself with one foot. "So who'd you tell about that morning in the office?"

I felt myself go absolutely cold. I looked around me. A deserted road, not even a car headlight in the distance. And beside the road a thicket of trees. "What morning?"

He began to pull off his gloves. "You know what morning. Don't play dumb. What did you hear and what did you tell?"

I looked for a place to run or somewhere to hide. In the moonlight Garth looked so fierce, that spiky haircut and the design he'd painted on his arm: a heart with a dagger through it, dripping blood. I looked at his hands. Biker's hands, the sinews of his arms like iron. He could have come back to the office in anger, found Miss Finister in the supply room, taken her throat in his hands. . . . He came toward me. "I'm not playing games, understand?" I moved backward toward the trees. Two more steps, his hands would be around my throat, and they'd find me in the thicket. . . .

I heard a bicycle skid to a stop. Over Garth's shoulder, I could see Mike in the moonlight. He jumped off his bike. It slid to the ground. Garth turned slowly. They were both about the same height, but Garth was tough, and Mike was not. "Leave her alone," Mike ordered.

Garth turned to face Mike, not disturbed at all, just amused, as Mike raised his arms in a fighter's stance and curled his hands into fists. He didn't much look like a fighter. Then suddenly he stopped, took off his glasses, and put them in his shirt pocket and repositioned himself. Too late. Garth was off his cycle. He shot out one quick jab, caught Mike on the nose. Mike's head flew back, he went off balance and over, onto the dirt, holding his hand up to his nose. Blood ran down his chin. Now Garth took a step closer, raised a boot to kick the fallen Mike.

I moved behind him. "Coward! Hitting a man when he's down! Try that on me!"

I guess I shocked him. He turned. I caught him off guard. Now you have to understand kick boxing. It's a beautiful, rhythmic kind of balance and movement. I'd been at it since I was six. When I trained, they made me count it out. One, fist forward; two, the other fist; three, kick; four, swing around and hit from behind. Only then it was into a leather pillow. I rarely worked out with bare flesh, always padded opponents. I happen to be very good.

He simply didn't expect me. It was almost too easy. I jabbed and caught him on the nose. The second jab caught him on the chin. The kick caught him in the stomach. He doubled over and fell to his knees. I didn't mean to hit him

that hard, but it was a lonely road and I was desperate—
the rest of the gang might be turning back.

"Let's ride!" I called to Mike. He was up on his bike,
his nose still dripping. I was up on mine. We made time!
If you could have clocked us, I swear we were making
record speed. Finally we saw the lights of Martindale. I
motioned toward the one place I knew we'd be safe.
Bozo's. The lights were on, most of the tables filled. We
dumped our bikes and ran inside. I mean, if you can't be
safe behind a clown with a big red nose, where can you?
There was one empty table. I looked toward the front
window to see if anyone was outside. Mike ordered a
couple of coffees and some cookies, just to make like a
customer. I went to the counter and asked for a glass of
water. I took a napkin and did some repair work on the
bloody nose. Mike winced and moved away from my
probing hand. He was looking at me, rather puzzled.
"Where did you learn to do that?"

"Do what?"

"What you did?"

"The fight, you mean? Well, even an airhead can be
good at some things."

He should have been gracious enough to say thanks, but
I think that his pride was a bit bent out of place. Still,
knowing that he was no match for Garth, he had tried to
save me. So I was the one who said, "Thanks. For coming
after me."

He reached tentatively to his battered nose. "Look, I
think it's fair to say that you and I, well, we don't get
along."

"Understatement of the year."

"But the fact is that Mr. Emerson is in deep trouble.
You know something. I may know something. And there's
a lot of investigation to do. The way it looks, they found
his fingerprints on her body, and Mr. Emerson hasn't said

anything, not even that he was innocent. So that means he
has some reason for not telling the truth. We can't let that
happen. We've got to go over everything, every clue, every
possibility, and save him before he does himself harm. And
if it means doing it together . . ." He took a deep breath. He
didn't exactly look me in the eye, he sort of avoided that.
He looked down at the cookies and at his hands. ". . . then
it's together."

"You mean partners."

"I mean partners until we solve this mystery."

"And after that we go our own ways."

"That's what I mean."

"So for now we're a team, right?"

His eyes were on the table, not on me. "Right."

"Okay." I bent closer. "I was in the office that morning.
There were three people who were furious with Miss Finister. One of them was Red Arnold. Miss Finister accused
him of cheating on his time card. He was going to be fired.
The second was Mr. Bragg. She implied that she saw him
'down by the river.' Whatever it was he did down there, he
was really upset about being seen. And the third was Garth
Meacham, who was getting suspended. So now we start
looking for proof that one of them hated Miss Finister
enough to kill her."

"Not Finister," he said. "Von Oster. I think her name
was Von Oster."

I almost overturned the water glass. "What?"

He looked around the room to be sure we weren't overheard. He leaned in closer to me. "I went out to Mr. Emerson's house about a month ago. He'd been telling me about
the time he was a foreign exchange student in England. He
was fixing a cup of cocoa. He told me to look upstairs in a
drawer of pictures, there were some good shots of the
House of Parliament. I came across a picture of him in

uniform, World War II. That was the war we fought with Germany."

I prickled. "I may not be exactly brilliant but I do know who we fought in World War II."

He leaned closer. "I was fascinated by the photo—I mean, he looked so young I could barely recognize him. And I'm interested because of my grandfather. He was a terrific athlete before he was wounded in the war. He caught a piece of shrapnel, and it ruined his whole life. Anyhow, I was looking at this picture when I realized that there was another photo stuck to the back. It was a pinup."

"Pinup?"

"The guys in World War II, they used to carry pictures of their favorite movie stars and they'd pin them up in their barracks or in their planes, for a touch of home. This really beautiful girl in a very short dance costume, lots of leg, all made up, smiling. It was signed Margo Von Oster. There was something about it that sort of buzzed me. I didn't know what it was. Her eyes, I guess. I didn't think any more about it until after the murder. Those eyes! Now, Miss Finister wasn't much of a beauty, she was a pretty bleak old lady, but she had almond-shaped eyes, really different eyes. And they were exactly the eyes of the girl in the photo. I know it sounds crazy. But this is forty years later. Margaret Finister. Margo Von Oster? I could swear they had the same eyes."

I shook my head. "No. I don't get it. If she was a beauty back in the old days, and he knew her then, and he still loved her, which frankly is hard to believe, then why . . . ?"

"I don't know. That's what we've got to find out. We've got to start at the beginning, asking questions."

"No," I said. "We've got to do something first."

"What's that?"

I pointed toward the window. I heard the roar of motors

as the whole gang began to pull up on cycles and park them outside. It was clear that they were waiting for us. "Okay. So we're a detective team. Mike and Ally. We're going to solve a crime and find out why Mr. Emerson let himself be accused of something he didn't do. But first of all, how on earth are we going to get out of here?"

4

They were just sitting there, about fifteen of them, looking at us through the window when a car pulled up next to them, my mother's car. Orville, still carrying that stupid bat, came running in, my mother close behind him, fuming. "Honestly, Allison, *hon*estly, we've been frantic worrying about you, we've been all over town, phoning your friends, and here you are all the time having a little—" She was going to say date.

"This is Mike Sloane. I rode out to his place to get some information about Mr. Emerson, and they"—I gestured to the window—"they followed us. We're afraid to leave."

Now, you have to know my mother. She's tall, very slim, very athletic (you see where I get my genes). She was once aboard a highjacked plane in Istanbul. She knocked out one of the armed highjackers and helped the captain to subdue the other. My mother is cool, I mean, *cool*. She stood for a moment glowering through the window, searching faces. "Mom!" Orville said, getting really nervous, putting the baseball bat behind him. "One of those guys, it's the guy Ally saw! You know!"

Now everyone was pretty much staring at us and at the wild bunch outside. Barry, who works the counter nights, asked if he should call the police. "Not necessary," my mother said. "I know one of those boys. I happen to play tennis with his mother. Look at him with his hair wild like that. Let's go."

Orville gave a little whimper. We all walked out, a little flock, led by my mother, who looked something like a Valkyrie, one of those ancient woman warriors. All of the wild bunch watch Garth for a sign. Garth was looking at me. My mother marched up to this unsuspecting Robert Michaels, I recognized him now, he'd spiked up his hair and changed his school sweater for a ragged shirt and he had tied a red bandanna about his head. "Robert," my mother said, "do you remember me? I used to carpool to drive you to nursery school. How is your mother? Please mention me to her."

He drove off like a bat out of you-know-where. About five of the others zoomed off. I couldn't do anything but follow her bravery. I walked up to Garth. "What did you want with me out there on the road? Were you going to knock me around or something?"

He gave a little snort of a laugh. "I told you what I wanted to know. All you had to do was answer me. Then Mike came up and tried to take a punch at me." He gunned his motor. "I know what you think," he said. "It's not true. So just don't do anything you might be sorry for."

My mother drove Mike back to Puddleston. "Are you safe there tonight? Don't you think it would be better if you spent the night with us?"

"Thanks, but my grandfather is blind. There's only the two of us. I have to get back to him."

So that's why he always left so fast after school, that's why he didn't go out for sports or anything.

"Then you'd better get a gun or something!" Orville exclaimed. "They're liable to come back in the middle of the night."

"Gun?" Mike said. "In our house? No way. My grandfather has a big thing about violence. Eye for an eye, he says. And the wars never stop. He had the job of gathering up abandoned arms after the war and he stepped on an unexploded shell."

"I'm so sorry," my mother said, "but, Mike, this is a violent world. You've got to protect yourself."

Mike got out of the car. "I hope that one day I'll be able to help find ways to solve problems without blowing anybody up. So thanks for the ride. I'll just get my bike out of the trunk."

I hopped out of the car and went with him. "It's only two weeks until the trial," he said. "We'd better get something really solid by then. After what just happened, Garth looks like a good place to start."

My head was filled with a thought that disturbed me. "Mike, I know what it looks like for Garth, especially after what he did this evening, but something tells me that he wasn't the one who killed her."

He wheeled his bike to the car and waited for me to get in. "Based on what?"

"Intuition."

He closed the car door for me. "If you want to work with me, you'll have to use something more solid. Intuition is an easy out. We need proof, not some silly girl's intuition." He walked the bike to the house.

"Well . . ." my mother said, in a tone that echoed my thoughts exactly.

All the warm feelings that spilled over me when I heard how he took care of his grandfather turned cold. "Silly girl? Is that what he thinks I am? I'll show him."

My mother drove onto the highway. She glanced over at me. I sat with my arms crossed, getting firmer and firmer in my resolve. I guess she knew that gesture. My father did just that when he was set on something. "Show him? I just bet you will."

5

Francine danced circles around me as we walked. "So what happened last night? It's all over town! You had a date with Mike? And Garth came after you?"

I walked with my nose bent into a notebook. Two columns. I labeled them *clear* and *hazy*. I guess I saw detective work sort of like Washington weather. Under the *clear* column, I had written:

Suspects.
Garth Meacham
Mr. Bragg
Red Arnold

Under the *hazy* I had written:

What did Miss Finister see down by the river?

36

I checked Garth's name. "Garth and his bunch hang out at the Green Zephyr sometimes, don't they?"

"What do you want with Garth! Ally, he's nothing but trouble!"

The Green Zephyr was way out on 14th Street. I'd have to hurry to make it there and back to school in time. "See you at lunch!"

I heard Francine calling after me. No time for small talk. This was detective work. By the time I saw Mike at school, I'd have a few answers. His eyes would open wide in amazement and then soften in admiration, and that afternoon he and I would take a walk down by the river, and as we sat on the melodious banks . . .

Green Zephyr, Leaded, Unleaded, and Diesel.

I saw Garth in jeans and a sweater pumping gas into a Ford station wagon. *He didn't just hang out there, he worked there!* I knew it! My intuition was right. I'd show Mike a thing or two.

He saw me as he was putting the money into the register. His eyes were on me as he cleaned off his hands. I didn't really know how to do this. Take the bull by the horns, my father always said. So I just walked up to him. "What were you trying to ask me last night?"

I saw him glance both ways to make sure we weren't being overheard. "You were there in the office. You know I was mad at old Finister. And you know my reputation, right?"

"I guess you try hard to keep up that reputation. Also right?"

He shrugged. "I couldn't have that suspension. I've applied for forestry school for next year. Well, maybe one suspension won't go against me. But if you tell the police about . . ." He swallowed hard. "They'll have me in as a suspect."

"But they arrested Mr. Emerson."

"That old guy? He didn't do it."

"How do you know?"

"I just don't think he did, that's all. So, are you going to tell them or not?"

I thought hard. He could have been trying to mislead me. But I am a pretty good judge of character. I didn't believe he was. "No, I won't say anything."

You could see how relieved he was. "It's been rotten with my father. You understand. I'm telling you this because you leveled with me. Getting a chance at the forestry service, it's my only way out."

I nodded. I understood. "Good luck," I said.

He actually smiled. He wasn't really that tough. "And you pack a mean kick," he said. "Take care, Ally."

I walked to school feeling jubilant. I couldn't wait to see Mike. I opened my notebook and crossed out the name Garth Meacham. The second name on my list was Bragg. And my intuition had plenty to say on that subject. All I had to do was prove it.

The office was a mess, kids milling around, Mr. Evanston himself at the desk trying to sort problems out. Mr. Bragg's door was closed. Bull by the horns. I knocked and went in.

Because this was my idea: To be a detective you've got to observe, watch for signs the way Mike's grandfather had done last night. I mean it, Mike was going to be so proud of me.

Mr. Bragg looked up, startled. Not only startled, but ragged, tired, as if he hadn't slept much the night before. "I think you wanted to see me? About the excuse? You remember? I thought I'd better get it over with now."

He wasn't focused yet. I could see by his face that something else was on his mind. And I was sure I knew what it was. "Sit down," he said.

He wasn't even thinking about me, old slimy Bragg and

his humiliating little ways. He was running his hand over the smooth surface of the new desk blotter. What really upset me was that he wore a school ring! Really Slimy. Trying to make Mr. Evanston think he had school spirit. And then he saw my eyes following his hands on the blotter. His forehead broke out into a sweat. *I saw that! That was a clue!*

He settled himself, trying to get that old Bragg look back on his face. "Well, Allison," he said finally, "I gather you have a little problem."

I had a vision of my mother facing down fifteen motorcycles. "Do I?" I asked Mr. Bragg. "Or do you?"

He knew exactly what I meant! His face flushed. His mouth twitched a little. *Okay, Mike Sloane. Am I a detective or not? This man looks guilty.*

His eyes bored into me, trying to figure me out. And suddenly he went all soft and smiling. "I gather you had your reasons for forging the note. Now mind you, I don't condone that sort of thing, but you've had a spotless record and let's not ruin it when you've only got one year to go. So let's say as a gesture, since I'm new at the job, that I grant clemency. Just don't let it happen again." He nodded that I was free to go.

The tardy bell rang. I was late. I ran.

Was I right or was I right?

I ran to English. English without poor Mr. Emerson there. I saw Mike waiting for me at the door. "I have something important to tell you."

"Later," he said. "And I've got something to tell you. Archery stacks. Noon."

We went inside and slipped into our seats. We had a sub, Mrs. Murchinson, who always loved to read "Thanatopsis." There was a general class moan as she opened the book, and we all settled down to a sleepy hour.

The bell woke us. Mike passed me going up the aisle. "Noon," he said.

Seconds stretched to minutes. I couldn't wait to see Mike's eyes when I gave him my brilliant deductions. When the lunch bell rang, I was off like a racehorse leaving the gate. The sports field is out beyond the school in a very large clearing near a thicket of trees. There's the stadium, the track, and, far beyond, the shot-putting and finally some old haystacks with targets where we practiced archery. I arrived before Mike and waited at the furthest stack. I was high with excitement, getting all my facts together to make my point.

Mike came across the field with that really serious look that meant he was trying to work out a problem. He leaned against the archery stack, perplexed. "I went down to the police station this morning. Marvin Letterman said that Miss Finister was wearing a plastic belt and some stone beads. There were fingerprints on both. Miss Finister had an office practice girl in there with her who said that nobody else was in the office that morning except the delivery man from the stationery supply who comes once a month. Miss Finister was putting the supplies away when she was strangled. They checked out the supply company. It was the same man they always use. The girl was out of the office for about fifteen minutes. When she came back, she saw the door open and Miss Finister dead. We know Mr. Emerson had an office summons during that time. He may have been in the office. But he didn't do it. We both know that. So then why were his fingerprints on the body?"

"And we've got three really good suspects. Well, two actually, because I don't think Garth did it. He'd been suspended, and he was mad at Miss Finister for not letting him back into class, but I spoke to Garth this morning.

Mike, we're wrong about him. He's basically a nice guy."

"Nice guy? That's why he almost broke my nose?"

"No, that was a mistake. You came at him and he was defending himself."

"Defending himself? That's why he tried to kick me when I was down?"

I deflated. I had forgotten about that kick. "But it's Bragg who's guilty! I'm sure of it. I went to the office this morning. I was in trouble for something I absolutely did. No question. But he was so afraid I'd tell that Miss Finister saw him 'down by the river,' he actually let me off! You should have seen him sweat! And now that I think of it, something else happened that morning. He asked Miss Finister for a new desk set, and she said, I mean ominously, as if he'd be out of a job soon, that he wouldn't be needing it! It was Bragg all right."

"It doesn't make sense, Ally. Why would a VP kill a secretary because she wouldn't give him a new desk set? And what was it she saw him doing down by the river? What goes on 'down by the river' anyway?"

"What? You know. Down by the *river*."

He frowned. "I don't know. If I knew, I wouldn't ask you."

So I guess he'd never been down by the river. "You know. Boy-girl stuff."

He blushed. He actually blushed. *Oh, Mike, look at me as if you see me. Let me show you the riverbank and the melodious shores.*

Now, Mike has rather longish blond hair, thick and curly. I'm not explaining this because I was thinking romance. I'm explaining this because if his hair had been shorter, he would have been dead.

Because as we spoke, an arrow came shooting through the air. It literally *parted* his hair and went *thud* into the stack. For a split second, I thought it had gone through his head. I screamed. He put his hand up, felt the arrow, a little pale himself, until he realized that it had missed his scalp.

Only then did I see the archer running across the yard, jumping the fence, and disappearing into the trees that thickly border the sports field. An archer with *red hair*!

"Then it isn't Garth or Bragg! That was Red Arnold!" I looked at the arrow in Mike's hand. "And I think that arrow must have been meant for me."

"Why do you think that?"

"Well, I'm the one who heard him in the office!"

"Heard who?"

"Red Arnold! Come on, you saw him yourself!"

"Saw what?"

"Red Arnold running with the bow in his hand!"

"I saw a man with red hair with a bow in his hand."

"Who else at Martindale High has red hair except Melvin Mason who's on the basketball team, and he's almost seven feet tall!"

"Think, Ally. Because this is getting more and more dangerous, and you've got to think clearly. What does Red Arnold look like?"

"Look! His back was toward us. We couldn't see his face. We only—" I stopped. Dumb. I was so dumb. It came to me in a flash. "Red is bow-legged. He walks in a rolling gait. And when he runs, he sort of lopes because he's heavy. The man with the bow was a fast runner."

"That's right," he said. "What I can't understand is why someone would try to take a shot at us and blame it on Red Arnold. There are too many whys. I've got to talk to Mr. Emerson and get some answers. I'm going to the courthouse after school and try to get in to see him."

"You mean that *we're* going to the courthouse."

He took his glasses off and cleaned them on his sweater. And then finally he *looked* at me. With his whole attention.

You know what I mean, *looked* at me as if he were really seeing me. "Ally, somebody just tried to kill one of us. It's too dangerous. You've got to get yourself out of this now."

I looked at the arrow. "You forget, I'm also a good archer. You start that "silly girl" stuff again, and you'll have two people trying to make a target out of you. We go together."

"You're sure you understand exactly what you're getting yourself into?"

"And you. You were the one he almost killed."

His eyes were really fierce. "It could have been you. Miss Finister is dead. Mr. Emerson's life is in peril. Somebody has got to stop this."

He was wonderful when he talked like that.

He put his glasses back on. He took up his notebook and opened it. I saw him write: *River, for romance.*

I only wish he meant me.

6

Martindale is very proud of its county courthouse with its two stone lions. They're really great lions, scowling fiercely, each holding one clawed paw over a fallen culprit and the other pawing the air, warning the wicked that justice will be done.

It's more than a courthouse because in the old days they actually had a jailhouse wing. Only now it's just for holding the accused until they're convicted and sent to Olympia or Seattle or somewhere.

I was thinking about those fallen culprits under the lions' paws as we climbed the worn stone steps. Mike was really upset. "Justice. Where's the justice in putting an innocent man like Mr. Emerson in a cell?"

We pushed open the heavy oak doors and stepped into the courthouse. The ceilings were high-vaulted and the floors were marble. We heard our footsteps echo as we walked. "The problem is," Mike said, "how are we going to get in to see him?"

"Easy," I said. "We'll tell them that we're a delegation to cheer Mr. Emerson up."

"That's ridiculous," Mike answered. "Just what a—"

"You keep this up, and you get your first lesson in kick boxing, here and now."

When a voice rang through the central hall calling "Mike Sloane!" we both stopped cold. Marvin Letterman's heavy shoes must have had cleats on them. They rang with musical tones as he hurried toward us. "Been looking all over town for you. Emerson wants to talk to you."

Mike and I looked at each other. "Me?" Mike asked. "Mr. Emerson asked to talk to *me*?"

"Don't you understand English?" Marvin broke into a high-pitched laugh. "English, get it? He was your English teacher, wasn't he?"

I felt like punching him out. "Is," I said, "not *was*. He's not guilty."

Marvin led us into the jailhouse corridor. "Isn't he?" he asked. "Looks pretty open and shut to me."

"Well, it's n—" Mike poked me hard. I was about to poke him back when I realized what I'd almost done: announced to the police that we were looking for the real murderer. Some detective. I guess I still had a lot to learn. Marvin opened a locked door with a key from his ring of keys. He squinted over at me. "He asked for Mike, not for you."

"It's okay. He meant both of us. Mike and I are working together."

Marvin had shifty squinty eyes. "Working on what?"

I saw Mike's mouth tighten. "We're up for a scholarship," I said, "and Mr. Emerson's been coaching us."

Marvin whistled through his teeth. He had a space between his two front teeth. "Up for murder, and he's still thinking of his kids. You can never predict about murderers."

"If he's a murderer," I said, "what about a motive?"

I thought for a moment I saw a squigeon of doubt. Only a moment. "Don't need a motive," Marvin said. "We have his fingerprints, don't we."

The door to the cell had a barred window. Through it I could see poor Mr. Emerson lying on a cot. Such a bleak little room, no furniture except his cot and one small rickety table. And one small rickety table. On that table, I could have cried when I saw it, was the dog-eared leather-bound volume of poems. The book with that sad poem in it.

"Visitors!" Marvin called.

I felt a cold sensation of dread as we walked into that little cell. Mr. Emerson looked up startled, first at Mike and then at me. It was Mike he wanted to see, not me. But he also wanted to get rid of Marvin without a fuss. I saw him nod. "Yes," he said. "Thank you."

The door closed.

"Are you all right?" Mike began.

Mr. Emerson waved Mike's words away as if the question were irrelevant. "There's something you must do for me, and quickly. I asked for you, Mike, because you're a young man of honor. I had hoped you'd do it alone. But Ally is here too, and I know Ally. I must trust the both of you."

"We're going to get you out of here!" I blurted. I felt so awful for him. "We'll find the real murderer if it's the last thing we do."

"No, you mustn't think of it!" he said. "There's too much danger. And"—his eyes were filled with shadows—"it doesn't matter now. Nothing matters. She's dead." He reached for the book, held it in his hands, ran a finger over the worn leather. "We were fools. We should have known from the first that it was hopeless."

We? Mike looked at me, I looked at him.

"Please, I must trust you both. There's very little time. I'm sure they've been all over the house by now. But if they'd found it, I'd know."

"Found what?" I asked.

Mike poked me.

We were an uneasy team. It was Mike's way to sit quietly, to listen, to take things in. Me, *on my tongue, into the air*, my mother always said. I'd have to get rid of that habit.

Mr. Emerson looked to the door to make sure we weren't being overheard. "In my study there is a small kilim rug, a most beautiful design. If you remember, Mike, I pointed it out to you." Mr. Emerson's eyes glazed over. "She and I, we bought it together. Our Persian adventure, we called it." He sighed deeply. "But that's over now. Under the rug, there is a parquet floor. Lift out the loose square. You'll find a small book. Burn it. Quickly. Now."

I started to ask the question that was on the tip of my tongue. Mike stopped me. "If that's what you want, yes. Immediately."

Mr. Emerson looked at us both, his eyes as bleak as death. "Thank you. Just take care of yourselves. Make sure that no one sees you entering the house." He shook Mike's hand and mine. "Good-bye," he said. There was such an air of finality about it, I wanted to hold him or hug him. But he'd already gone back to the cot and lay down with an arm across his eyes.

"But I've got to ask one question!" Mike tried to stop me. I shook him off. "We know you're not guilty. But your fingerprints were all over her. Why?"

He never took the arm from across his eyes. He answered almost mechanically, as if it were an old story not worth telling. "I had an office summons that morning, you remember. Margaret had something important to tell me. I found the storeroom door open. We often met in there, for a few moments, when things got too heavy for us. I found her there, crumpled on the ground, dead. At first I couldn't believe it. We had waited so long. I thought we'd escaped them, that we were free at last. When I saw her lying there . . . when I realized what she'd given up for that dream . . . I had to hold her and say good-bye. I had to tell her that I would love her for eternity."

And then silence. Nothing more.

We called to be let out.

Outside, we stood at the base of one of the lions, both of us shaken. "What did he mean about 'waited so long'? So long for what?"

"That," Mike replied, "is what we're going to find out. And I have a feeling that it's in the book he wants us to burn."

"Feeling?" I said, with the greatest satisfaction. "Do you mean that you're relying on intuition?"

I didn't expect an answer. And I imagine I was smiling a smug little smile, the one that Allan Alderman, who made the basketball All-stars last term, called my killer smile.

But Mike wasn't in the mood to notice it.

Mr. Emerson lived in a pretty little cottage out on East Street. We both turned in that direction and ran.

7

The door was locked. Mike and I circled the house until we found a small basement window unlatched. We dropped down onto a mountain of old furniture, paint cans, and musty tarps, then made our way up the dark basement steps and into the house. I had been there once, with an English class for "high tea," as Mr. Emerson called it, very British, during the unit on Victorian literature.

Mike held me back. "Someone's been here."

I looked at the room. I didn't see anything.

"The chair, at the dining-room table. Been moved and put back out of place. And look there."

Now I saw it. A drawer in the sideboard opened, searched, papers shoved back in but a few edges showing and the drawer not quite closed. We moved through the room toward the stairs. We climbed slowly, listening to make sure we were alone in the house.

We walked down the hallway toward the study. It was

the largest and best room in the house. We'd had our class tea up there. I remembered his shelves of books, his wonderful engravings, the statues of Shakespeare and Dickens, his records and tapes. The door was ajar. Mike pushed it open. The light was beginning to fade. We didn't need much light to see what had happened.

Every drawer had been opened and dumped onto the floor. Every book on every shelf opened and thrown aside. Every engraving had been taken down and turned over. Newspapers, magazines, opened, scattered. The desk drawer had been dumped on a table, papers flung everywhere. Even the back of the drawer had been broken out, looking for secret compartments, I supposed.

"The Martindale police are pretty heavy-handed," Mike said, "but they wouldn't leave a mess like this."

Mike went to the table where the drawer had been dumped. He rummaged through scattered papers until he found the photo he wanted. "Look," he said. I could hardly believe it was Mr. Emerson. A smiling young man in uniform, very handsome, his hat tipped rakishly back on his head. But it wasn't that photo Mike wanted to show me. He turned it over. Stuck to the back was the pinup! Even in the fading light I could see how beautiful she was, that long silken hair curling over her shoulders. She wore a two-piece forties-style bathing suit. She posed seductively: shoulders back, lots of leg in high-heeled shoes. I took the photo to the window, held it up to the last of the light. No, Mike was mistaken. It wasn't her nose at all, nor her chin. It was only the odd resemblance of the eyes, almond-shaped eyes, very far apart, and high arched brows. I could see how he could have thought . . . the eyes were really different. And they were exactly Miss Finister's eyes. The photo was signed Margo Von Oster. Mike tucked the pinup into his jacket. "Let's find the book."

Under all that mess were three rugs. "Which rug?"

"The kilim."

"What's a kilim? They all look like Persian rugs to me. Where is Persia, anyway, where they had their adventure?"

"There isn't any Persia."

"What do you mean isn't any? I know Persia. Like the *Arabian Nights* and stories like that. Didn't they talk about Persia?"

He walked to the small rug in the center of the floor. "Persia was the old name. It's Iran now. Those other two, they're Orientals. This one is a kilim. He told me about it once when I was here. Nomadic tribes used them on the floors of their tents, very colorful and each one original. He really made a point of telling me. Do you think the book was on his mind even then?"

We flipped back the corner of the rug. The parquet floor was made of small squares glued together in a pattern. Mike ran his hand over the surface. He felt carefully at all the cracks. "Here it is." One of the squares was loose. He pushed on one side of it until the other side edged up and then got his fingers under it. This was so exciting! I loved being a detective and searching out clues. I watched Mike pull out the wooden square and reach his hand into the hole. He took out a book. But not the kind of book I expected. There was nothing on the cover or on the spine. It was more of a diary!

It was then we heard the sound. Mike froze, the diary in one hand, the other held palm-up to me for silence. I happen to have sharp hearing. I can detect "Awful" coming into my room to get at my "extra money" tray even when he's barefoot and holding his breath. There was a creaking of boards out in the hall.

Someone was out there!

I saw Mike's eyes go around the room. So did mine. There were two windows, one to the front of the house, one to the side, which opened onto the roof. Hanging over the roof was a high oak tree.

Mike pointed to the side window. I could hear creaking again. We moved as silently as we could toward the window. Mike opened it. I stepped out onto the roof. He climbed after me and lowered the window.

The shingles were sloped and slippery. I slid down the roof to a branch of the oak. I turned back to see Mike edging very slowly down the shingles. Now, I happen to love danger. When things get exciting, I pump adrenaline. It clears my head. Mike knows kilim and all that, but he didn't know doodley about danger. I motioned for him to hurry. Nervously he edged down the shingles. I bent over the roof, caught a branch of the tree, went hand over hand toward the trunk, got my shoe onto a good footing and worked my way down. I waited for him at the bottom.

He was perched at the edge of the roof trying to get onto a sturdy branch. He found one, tested it. I could see that he didn't have good spatial judgment. I do. Got it from both my parents. My father can put a ball in a basket ten out of ten. My mother golfs like a pro. I was urging Mike to hurry now because I saw a face at the window. The window was dusty, it was getting dark, the face was blurred. Mike was a bit below his vision. I couldn't tell if he could see Mike or not.

Mike grabbed the branch, started hand over hand toward the trunk. But he was heavier than I was. I heard the squeaking of the branch as it started to break. It dipped, lower and lower. He was about eight feet above the ground as the branch cracked. Mike hit ground on a mass of leaves. Dogs began to bark up and down the street.

Mike lay on the grass, evidently using some very strong language under his breath. He got to his feet. He winced, he'd hurt his ankle. I made a quick survey of the bones with my fingers. I'm good at sports accidents. We've had enough of them in our family. "Not broken, just twisted. Let's get out of here."

We went over two fences, and down the road.

Where were we? About five blocks from the river. There was a thicket down there, very dense. "Come on!" He was favoring the hurt ankle as he ran. The light was fading fast. We cut across Downdale Street to River Road and down that to the riverbank. We slid down the bank and walked the muddy river path. We'd had some rain that week. "Here," I said. "This way."

In that thicket was a marvelous old burned-out tree. Ground fire had gutted away the whole inside. But the back was still there. It made a kind of cave. A wonderful hiding place, or a place to be alone. We both crowded in. "Goose pen," said Mike.

"What?"

"They used to call these goose pens. These burned out holes in trees. Good place to keep the geese and chickens dry." He sat on the damp ground and felt at his ankle. "I know so much trivia," he said. "But when real trouble comes, what good am I? I guess it was the way Grandpa brought me up. Because of his accident. He made one bad step, and it ruined his whole life. And when my folks died in that car crash, there was nobody but him to raise me. I guess he just wants to keep me safe."

"When was that? The car accident, I mean?"

"I was about eight. I've lived with Grandpa almost all my life. I'm his eyes. He's taught me everything, how to look at things and describe them, how to study, how to learn." Mike took the book out of his pocket. Slowly he opened the cover. We could see the familiar handwriting. We'd seen it on the board often enough. There was something written on the front page. We held the book up to what was left of the light. There were four words:

UFYR JGNQ KW JGNQ

I could see Mike's hand clutching the book. "What he didn't teach me was how to handle trouble. Because we've got trouble now. I thought we could take a quick look and then burn it. But the book is in code. So what do I do?"

"We take it home and decode it. We read it. We have to. His life is at stake."

"It's not only the matter of the promise to burn it. But taking it home means that whoever wanted it is still out there looking."

We sat for a long while beside that wonderful river with the music of water on rocks and the little breeze that made the trees whisper. The night was soft. We sat so close our shoulders touched. Suddenly I felt him shiver. "Ally, I think he really meant for me to read it."

"How? How do you know that?"

He climbed out of the goose pen. "It's late. I can't leave Grandpa any longer. I'll take you home and then catch a ride out to Puddleston."

I edged after him. "But not without me."

"Ally, this is a code I have to work out, and a code is mathematical, and you can't even manage algebra. We were in the same class, remember?"

The night, the sounds of the river, him so close, and he had to mention algebra. I felt my high spirits deflate.

He actually put his arm around me. "I'm sorry. I just don't know how to talk to people. I've been alone so much." He lifted my chin so that my eyes met his. He bent down to me, close, closer. I thought . . . *now* . . . *with the sound of the river and the wind in the trees*. And then he moved back. "I'd better take you home."

"Look," I said, "maybe I can't do algebra, but I helped to find the book with you and I want to be there when you read it. We'll catch a ride together. I'll call home from your place."

I was forbidden to hitchhike, but in case of dire emergencies, my father taught me how to judge "selective" transportation. We climbed back up to River Road. Mike's ankle was pretty sore by now. He leaned on my shoulder as he hobbled. Three or four cars passed us. And then I heard Mr. Wendall's truck coming down the road. Mr. Wendall drained cesspools. His truck had transmission trouble. I remember him explaining to my mother when he was out at our house last spring that the truck always got stuck in first gear. It made a noise like a cement mixer. I got out onto the road and waved my hands. He wheezed to a stop. All the equipment in the truck jingled and bumped. He peered out. "It's me! Ally McNeil! You were out at our house on Vernon Lane. You remember my father, the airline pilot?" He peered down at Mike. "My friend hurt his ankle. We need a ride up to Puddleston. Can you help us out?"

He had all this junk on the seat so we had to jump up in back. Now, a truck that's used to clean cesspools isn't the most fragrant ride. In fact, it was pretty awful. We were both trying to breathe shallowly. I had my sweater pulled up over my nose. No help. Mr. Wendall dropped us off near the house. It was really dark now. We ran up the long path to the stand of rhododendrons. Suddenly Mike stopped and held me back. "What is it?"

"The house. It's dark."

"Why would your grandfather turn on the lights if he can't see? Why shouldn't it be dark?"

"Lights are on a timer. So that if I come home late, I can find my way onto the porch. Something is wrong. Wait here."

Not on anybody's life was I going to wait there.

Mike walked up the steps cautiously. The door was open. "Grandpa?" he called. No answer. I edged up behind

him. He reached in and turned on the light. He held me
behind him so he saw the room first. He gasped.

Chairs had been pushed over, drawers pulled out,
papers flung around, cupboards opened. "Grandpa!" he
called. He was really frightened now. So was I. He ran
down a hallway that was strewn with feathers. Someone
had cut open all the pillows. He threw open his grandfather's bedroom door. The bed had been slashed, all the
stuffing out of it. And then I heard Mike cry out,
"Grandpa!" Mike fell to his knees beside the sprawled
body of the blind old man.

8

Mike was in shock, I could see that. I felt the old man's wrist. Heart beating, not strong, but beating. I looked for blood. None. Just an awful lump on the old man's head. I shook Mike. "He's alive. He's all right. Just knocked out."

Mike came up out of his shocked trance-like state with a gasp and a cry. He took his grandfather up in his arms. "Grandpa, what have they done to you!"

I was more practical. I went for a cold cloth, put it on the swollen lump, patted the old man's wrists and face. We heard him moan. His eyelids fluttered. "Grandpa, it's me," said Mike, eyes filled with tears. "You're all right now."

Across the old man's face, a flickering smile. "Sounds like Mike, smells like a . . . I won't say what."

We lifted his grandfather to the bed, but he didn't want to lie down, he wanted to sit up. He wanted to feel Mike's face and mine. "Must have given you both a turn."

"Whoever did this, I'll kill him!" Mike said fiercely.

The old man reached up a hand to touch Mike's cheek. "Never, never let me hear you say that. An eye for an eye, that's half destroyed this world. I've taught you to find other solutions. Whoever hurt me, you search them out and bring them to justice."

The look on Mike's face. I knew him well enough to read it now. I knew that his life's work had been set for him by the old man he loved, and I also knew at that moment that he'd never rest until somebody paid not only for Margaret Finister and Mr. Emerson but for the old man he held in his arms. "Grandpa, why?" Mike asked. "Everyone out here knows you don't have much money. Why did they do this?"

"There were two of them," said his grandfather. "They wanted to know where you had hidden the book. What book, Mike?"

Mike took the diary out of his pocket. He winced as he looked at his grandfather's bruised head and at the destroyed house. He put the small black book in his grandfather's hands.

His grandfather inspected the book with his fingers. "What is this book and why is it important enough for someone to do violence to get it?"

"That's what we don't know," I said. "Mr. Emerson told us to find it and burn it. We think it might contain a clue to whoever killed Miss Finister. We were going to read it first, but it's in code."

His grandfather rocked a bit, thinking. "What sort of code?"

"On the first page," Mike said, "are four word groups. Three four letters. One two letters. And one group repeated. Grandpa, I won't risk your life and Ally's any longer. Mr. Emerson said that the book was dangerous and to burn it. I'm going to burn it now."

Mike tried to take the book, but his grandfather held it

tightly. "He meant for you to read it. You know that."

Mike nodded seriously, his eyes on his grandfather, that look of worry still engraved on his face. "Yes, Grandpa, I know."

It was infuriating. "How could he know and how could you know that Mr. Emerson wanted you to read it when *I* don't know!"

"He knows," said Mike, "because he worked for a while in cryptology early in the war."

"Crypt-what?" I said.

"'Kryptos,'" Mike said. "Greek for 'hidden.' 'Logos' for 'word.' Hidden words. And Grandpa knows that creating a serious code is a complicated matter with all the new electronic equipment they have now. No serious code would be written in sections of different lengths. Gives away too much. And to repeat a word is a real giveaway. And he also knows that I told Mr. Emerson about his interest in codes. No, it was meant for me to read."

"But Mr. Emerson said, I remember absolutely that he said he wanted you because you were a man of honor. Doesn't honor mean that he wanted you to burn it?"

Mike looked to his grandfather, his eyes swamped with concern. "Grandpa, he meant for me to read it. And then he meant as a man of honor that I would burn it. I'm sure the book explains why he's not defending himself for the murder. That means I'll know but won't act. And more than that, this is a dangerous thing to keep in the house. Danger, do you understand, Grandpa? You taught me to be cautious, to use my brains, to fight violence with logic. But what if a fight means not only brains but fists? What if somebody I love is in peril? Do I jump in and fight then? Is that senseless violence, too?"

The old man paled. He shrank back, inward and thinking. That was a hard question. Mike put an arm around the old man and held him close. "We'll figure it out, Grandpa.

You and I. Now let's work out the code. Let's find the key. We haven't much time."

"Key!" I said. "How can you find a key! I mean, there must be hundreds of things that could be a key."

"You must think," the old man said patiently. To me. Mike was already thinking, I knew the signs. "Consider the man who wrote the code. What was his state of mind when he wrote it? That narrows down your keys. What would be important to him?"

I loved the way the old man thought. Here, in this mad room with feathers all over the place, mirrors broken, his own head probably throbbing, and he was thinking of logical solutions. I had so much to learn. "Well, Mr. Emerson was worrying about Miss Finister. And the day after she was found dead, right before the police came to arrest him, he read us a poem from this favorite old dog-eared copy of Edna St. Vincent Millay." It was all popping into my head now. "And when we saw him in his jail cell, he had a copy of that book next to his cot!"

"Not bad," Mike said. "I can see from her eyes that she's figured it out, Grandpa."

"You know what the key is! You've already figured it out!"

"Sure. So can you. Maybe you mess up in algebra, but you're not bad at thinking things through. What's the code?"

I actually had a compliment from Michael Sloane! Did I know what the code was? Yes, I did know! Mr. Emerson sat in front of the class grieving over the death of his beloved. The words he read were "What lips my lips have kissed" . . . four words, we repeated, one of two letters. *What lips my lips!* "It's the poem!"

"The poem," said Mike. "It's a child's code. You take each letter, count back or forward a certain number of letters of the alphabet, and make a substitution." He took his grandfather's hand. "If you're sure you're all right, I'll get to work. Before this night is over, we'll know who Margo Von Oster really is."

Mike's grandfather raised his eyebrows. "Margo Von Oster? Why didn't you ask me? I can tell you who Margo Von Oster is, or was. You don't need to decode a book for that."

Mike looked worriedly at me. Had the blow on the head done something awful? "Grandpa, how could you know a thing like that?"

"How could you not know if you were a soldier in the European campaign of the Second World War? Margo Von Oster was a German actress who broadcast on the radio. It was all we could get most of the time, her voice, singing to us, talking to us in low seductive tones, reminding us how much we missed our loved ones back home, how wrong we were to fight and die for causes that weren't our own." He sighed deeply. "I can see her face now. The Germans used to drop photos from planes. They were scattered everywhere."

"But what happened to her?" I said. "I mean, after the war?"

"After the war they discovered she was not only an actress helping to destroy Allied morale, she was a spy as well. I think they shot her."

Mike reached into his jacket and pulled out the now-wrinkled photo of the beautiful girl with the odd almond-shaped eyes. "Grandpa, I can swear that the eyes of Margo Von Oster are the eyes of Margaret Finister. But if Margo Von Oster was shot after the war, how could she have been working behind the desk in the front office of Martindale High?"

9

I had phoned home to tell my mother I had some study-ing to do with Mike, and that I'd really appreciate it if she'd pick me up much later that night. She said she was delighted that I had taken an interest in homework and that the latest she could pick me up would be nine, Orville wasn't too keen on staying alone in the house, ahem. Great. Nine would be fine. That would give us two hours.

Mike was already in his room working out the pages. I had started to clean up that mess while Mike's grandfather, who said that he felt better except for a headache, went into the kitchen to make us both some tea. It was marvel-ous to see how a blind man could do things for himself. He set the cups of fragrant tea on the cleaned-off table, then motioned me to sit beside him. "I'm afraid I've been a great trouble to Mike. I'm so happy he's found a friend like you, Allison. He's been rather isolated because of me."

"He's more than a friend, he's . . . so wonderful. . . ." I

shouldn't have said that to his grandfather! "I mean," I floundered, "what I meant to say was . . ."

"Child," he said with so much feeling, "don't ever be shamed by your emotions. To love someone is a blessing. It's hate that's destroying the world. Mike's father and mother died so young. I'm all he's known of love." He smiled. "And poor Mike, when other parents were reading nursery rhymes and picture books, I was teaching him logic."

The hot tea was good. "We aren't too logical in my family," I said. "We trust our instincts. My father says that you always know the truth at gut level."

"It's not bad to trust your instincts if they're founded on good observations. Look at Sherlock Holmes. He had an astonishing intuition about criminals. But his fantastic conclusions were only keen observation. He looked at a man's hands and deduced his line of work. He looked at the heels of his shoes and figured out where he walked each day. He watched a criminal stop to read a sign and deduced what thoughts the sign conjured up in his head." He sipped at his tea. "I made a few observations of my own when the men were . . . shall I say, questioning me. Both of them tried very hard to speak only in hoarse whispers."

"They didn't want their voices recognized!"

"That's right. Meaning it was someone I might have heard before. And one of them was younger, one was older."

"But how could you know that if you couldn't see them or really hear their voices?"

"When they touched me. I felt their arms. A young arm has a certain skin texture, an older arm has a certain muscle tension. One was stocky, one was slim. And one was more compassionate than the other. He tried more than once to make his partner stop hitting me. They had a whispered argument when I said I knew nothing about the book. One wanted to leave. The other struck me again and again."

I shuddered. "I can't believe that right here in Martindale, people we know and probably trust would murder a school secretary and hit a helpless man."

He shook his head sadly. "Child, the world is full of deception. We must uncover it, and find our own way to fight it. Mike's is through knowledge."

Now I knew what it was that attracted me to Mike. He didn't just *look* like Clark Kent, he was being trained to *be* Superman. Not flying through the sky, Mike wasn't much of a flyer, but as a beam of light in the dark of evil.

The old man put down the cup. "Something else. It just came to me. When I was out there in the kitchen making tea, the teapot had been moved. I'm used to everything in its place. Instead of touching it, my hand glanced against it. I wear this ring." He showed me a school ring. "It made a sound like *ping*, like hitting a ring against metal. When one of them was tying me up, I heard a sound like that. *Ping*."

All right. I could be logical, like Sherlock Holmes. There were two men: one younger, one older; one heavier, one lighter. Well, Mr. Bragg was younger, Red Arnold was older. Mr. Bragg was thinner, Red Arnold was heavier. And then came the haze again. Here was a hidden book written in code. It was important enough for somebody to want to kill for it. It was important enough for a man to let himself be tried for a crime and not to defend himself.

So what on earth would a crummy vice principal and an ex-rodeo maintenance man know about a book like that?

"Feeling tired now," Mike's grandfather said. "Think I'll lie down."

He stretched out on the sofa near the fireplace. I covered him with a little lap rug. Soon I heard his breathing, deep and even.

I leaned against the sofa, half watching the flame's shadows on the wall. I may have dozed. I woke when Mike touched my arm.

He spoke softly. He didn't want to wake his grandfather. "It was only ten pages, Ally. He wrote it the night after she was killed. He wrote it so that someone else would know the truth about him and Margo Von Oster." He looked into the fire. The light from the burning logs gave his face a kind of glow. "It only makes me realize more how stupid war is. How crazy men are to try to solve their problems by killing each other. He loved her so much, and no matter what they tried to do to be together, war kept them apart right to the end."

I turned down the lights so that Grandpa could sleep. I sat very close to be able to hear. I didn't want to miss a word.

"Mr. Emerson was so much like Grandpa. A scholar. He really cared about human life. And then he got drafted. He told them he couldn't, in all good conscience, kill a man. So they put him in a back room somewhere in Europe deciphering codes for Army Intelligence."

"Intelligence? Doesn't that mean spying?"

"He was just a quiet guy who worked alone in a closed room. For years until the war was almost over. The Germans were finally being beaten. They badly needed oil to run their tanks. And they found that someone had discovered a formula for synthetic fuel. Maybe they killed the guy to get it, I wouldn't doubt it, but it went hand to hand, and eventually it was on its way back to Germany. The Americans found out who was carrying the formula. A man and his woman companion, working as actors entertaining the Nazi troops. He calls the man Franz and the woman was—"

"—Margo Von Oster!"

Mike moved closer to me so that he could keep his voice low. "Margo Von Oster.

"The Americans had to get the formula. But they really weren't certain that Franz and Margo had it. They sent someone from Intelligence to find out. But they couldn't send a trained spy. Franz was too sharp. Franz and Margo were in Casablanca working in a night club. So the Americans sent a conscientious objector posing as an ambulance driver for the Red Cross. Casablanca was an open city. He was there on a rest leave. He went to this club and heard Margo sing. He asked her to dance . . ."

". . . and fell desperately in love."

"She wasn't a spy. She was a young actress. The Nazis had forced her into broadcasting to the troops. They'd threatened her with death unless she helped get that formula back to Germany. She detested the Nazis. When she met Mr. Emerson, she was at the end of her rope. His love was the only thing that saved her from killing Franz and then killing herself. She and Mr. Emerson met in secret and made their plans. They drugged Franz and escaped."

"But the formula!"

"They had to take it with them."

"Because if the Germans got it, they might have won the war! So why didn't they just go back to the Americans and turn themselves in?"

"She was afraid. She was sure they'd try her as a spy. Her voice, her face were known to every American soldier. How could they just let her go? He thought they'd execute her, just to make a point. You know how Mr. Emerson felt about war. He was afraid that certain grasping men would get hold of the formula. Certain countries desperately need oil, and other countries sell oil. One side would kill to get the formula, the other side would kill to destroy the formula. More war. More killing. They didn't know what to do. So they just ran and took the formula with them."

"Where?"

"South America, drifting down jungle rivers until the war was over. Africa. Remember Emerson said they had a 'Persian' adventure? Then they got tired of running. He wanted to go home. So they had to find a way to take new identities and get back to the States."

The truth hit me so hard it hurt my heart. "They could get false passports, get into the States somehow, he could change his hair, grow a beard, but she was a known beauty! A million servicemen knew her face!"

Mike touched a strand of my hair as if he were thinking of poor Margo. He ran his fingers along my cheek and around my chin. "She had her nose changed and her chin. She made herself plain so that she could stay with him."

I searched my own heart. Could I have done that for love? "So they went back to the States?"

"She had family in Minnesota. They got her in. She worked as a secretary for two years before he was able to come. He got a job as a teacher. They never spoke, never met for almost a year. They waited to make sure nobody was following them. They thought they were safe. And then one day they were walking down the street and out of the corner of her eye she saw a face. She almost died of shock."

I felt the chill of fear. "Franz!"

He writes that Franz was like a devil. They left town, he one way, she another. They didn't meet again for a year. And then two years in a small town, until they were certain he'd never find them. And then he turned up again. That's what life has been for them: running, hiding. Then a few years together."

"And finally they came to Martindale!"

"And Franz didn't turn up. For almost ten years. Finally they felt safe and sure. Franz might even have died by then. And they were getting old. Mr. Emerson was about to retire, buy a little place somewhere where it was warm. She would retire next term and follow. It had to be now or never. Because he still adored her, but poor Margo—"

"—she'd become tired and hard and bitter. That's why she acted so mean. But who killed her? There was no old Nazi hanging around Martindale High! People would have noticed! And the formula! What happened to the formula?"

He held up the little black book. "Here. The story is just meant as an explanation. The formula is here in the book." He took one last look at the book and tossed it into the fire.

10

The fire ignited the cover. It smoldered and then the pages caught. The cover bubbled as the pages became a little hot heart of flame, like the heart of a beautiful woman who had changed herself into a plain, sad, old lady to be with the man she loved. In the end she lay in his arms, but only in death.

The book was ashes now. I watched Mike poke at them with the fire tongs. "But that formula, it must be worth millions."

"More than mere millions," Mike's grandfather said. He hadn't been sleeping, just lying there with his eyes closed. He'd heard it all. "That formula could change the face of the world, bring energy to energy-starved nations."

"But we should have kept it!"

Mike shook his head. "It would also mean the end of the oil industry, the fall of nations."

"And Mike knows very well what men of power would

give for that formula. Nations that lived on oil, they'd kill to destroy it. Men who wanted to control the world, they'd deal for it. And wars might be fought over it. Now you know why a school secretary in an obscure town in Washington state was murdered."

When we heard the knock at the door we all jumped. Mike quickly moved to his grandfather, ready to defend him with his own life. Me, I'm more practical. I looked around for a weapon, took the fireplace poker. We saw the doorknob turn. I stood near the door, the poker raised high. The door opened a few inches. A baseball bat poked in, then Orville's head. "Ally?" My mother pushed Orville into the room.

I put the poker down. "Sorry, just a little nervous about what's been going on, I guess. Thanks for coming so late. We really had important work to do." I looked to Mike. "I guess we'll have to figure out what to do next. Mr. Emerson's trial is only a couple of weeks away."

My mother introduced herself to Grandpa, since none of us was polite enough to do it. "There won't be a trial, I'm afraid," she said. "Honey, I couldn't tell you over the phone. I thought I'd better tell you and Mike in person. Marvin Letterman came by about an hour ago looking for you. He had sad news. He knew how concerned you were about your English teacher. I'm afraid that the strain was simply too much for Mr. Emerson. When they brought him his dinner tonight, they found him dead."

Mike pulled his grandfather closer. I knew what was in his heart. Everyone he cared about, his parents, almost his grandfather, now Mr. Emerson, gone.

I really wanted to comfort Mike. But not here and not now.

We drove home through the moon-filled night. Orville was tired. He climbed into the back seat to stretch out. "Everything all right?" my mother asked me.

How could I answer? My heart was filled with smoke and ashes, with an old sad story, with the memory of a wonderful teacher and his lost love.

And with something else. If Mr. Emerson had died in jail, why would Marvin Letterman come all the way up to the house to tell me? Why didn't he just phone? And why would he have wanted to tell me at all so late at night? Why wouldn't he just wait until tomorrow?

"How come Red Arnold is all the way up here?" Orville asked.

My head was spinning. "What?"

"Red Arnold. He drives this panel truck with the weird license. It reads ABC223. It's a neat one. Every time I see the truck, I say ABC223. I like licenses that have rhymes in them. Like ours is YZU812."

I turned to look at Orville, who was curled up with his baseball bat. "Are you sure?"

"He was parked out there just behind some trees on the road. And when we drove off, his car lights went on. I guess he's still behind us."

There were a pair of headlights behind us. They turned off on a side road. We drove home in darkness.

That night I lay awake for a long while.

I thought about a young actress who gave up her beauty for the man she loved. I thought about Mike who had been taught his whole life to stay away from danger, and yet on the dark road when Garth threatened me, he'd put up his fists to fight. I thought of Mike on the archery court, holding that arrow in his hand and still determined to go on and find the murderer of Miss Finister. I thought I was the one with courage. I could jump out of a plane, I could face a big bully with my fists and my feet. But there was another kind of courage. Mike's kind. I thought about that. And I thought about Mike's wonderful eyes. . . .

11

Francine was having a cup of cocoa and some toast as I came down. "Hurry. You haven't got much time."

I rubbed my eyes. "Isn't it Saturday? No school."

My mother took her cup of coffee up to bed. She never had Saturday breakfast downstairs when Daddy wasn't home. Her chance to be lazy, she said. "Honey, Francine thought that you might want to go, since he meant so much to you."

I poured myself some cocoa. "Go where?"

"They're burying her today," said Francine. "Old dead Miss Finister."

Orville dragged in wearing his baseball PJ's. "They wouldn't be burying her if she wasn't dead, *Fran*cine." He talked that way in the morning. He was particularly acid first thing in the morning. I think he had bad dreams when Daddy was away.

"And you heard about poor Mr. Emerson. They're

burying him, too. I guess that since they have the cemetery opened up, they might as well kill two birds—" She gulped her cocoa. She must have remembered how I felt about Mr. Emerson. "Sorry, I'm such a glomp. You want me to go with you? I'm not too good at graveyards. I'll walk you to the bottom of Cemetery Hill. It's pretty spooky outside today. I could barely find your house in the fog."

"Thanks, no. I guess I'll want to be alone. I can't believe he's dead. I guess his heart just couldn't stand it."

"It wasn't his heart." Francine looked at the plate of blueberry muffins my mother had set out on the table. She reached for one, then she pulled her hand back and sighed deeply. "He didn't die of a heart attack. Didn't you hear? It's all over town. That's why they're burying him so fast. Martindale has had more awful things happen in these last couple of weeks than in the last two hundred years. He hanged himself. I guess he couldn't stand the shame. Or else maybe he really killed her and his guilt overcame him."

Francine walked me to the bottom of Cemetery Hill. I started up alone. The morning was eerily shrouded. Coastal Washington often gets like this: heavy mists hanging over the ground, a thin white veil of wet gook that makes the trees so gloriously green and the rocks moss-covered.

Martindale built its cemetery on the only hill, to bring people closer to heaven, I guess. It's a very old cemetery, dating back to pioneer days. I love to walk through, in hot summer when the sky is bright, and read the gravestones. "Be ye also ready." "Here lies Albert Fell, he died when he slipped bending over a well." They used a lot of what my father calls "gallows humor" in the pioneer days. Walking the cemetery in the wet season is really scary. I mean, someone walks at you through the mist and you don't know. . . . I could see the shadowy outlines of a figure now.

I don't believe in ghosts. *But there was worse than a ghost in Martindale. There was a man so crazy he'd shoot an arrow out on a school field in plain sight of practically anyone!* I stopped. I listened. I got myself ready for an evasive action. I heard Mike's voice. "Ally? Is that you?"

I practically fell into his arms.

"You heard the way he died," Mike said. "They hounded him to death. They killed the only thing he had to live for."

We climbed the foggy hillside. "Last night," I said, "Orville swears he saw Red Arnold's car parked near your place."

"And I saw muddy footprints on the porch this morning. I think he may have run up on the porch and seen us throw the book into the fire, because nobody else bothered us last night. So I guess that Red Arnold is involved."

"So it's Bragg and Red Arnold, then!"

"Ally, we can't jump to that conclusion. Red Arnold may have been on the porch. *May.* But what proof do we actually have that Bragg was involved with the murder? We don't know what happened *down by the river.*"

We walked through the whitish, thickish fog. He was actually holding my hand, guiding me over rocks and around gravestones. We were connected. I have to tell you the truth. Even cold and wet, that hazy veil of white shrouding us from the whole world, with his hand holding mine I felt the heat of summer.

The hearse began to climb the hill behind us. The Martindale Funeral Parlor has only one hearse, and it has a muffler problem. Whenever there's a funeral, the whole town knows, because the muffler roars and coughs. Now it had reason enough to cough. It was carrying two coffins. Maybe Mike was thinking that too as it passed. He pressed my hand. The two lovers. The young soldier, and the actress who gave her beauty to be with him. Together finally, but only in death.

And then another car passed. The only Martindale taxi, I could see the patch of yellow through the haze. "Mr. Emerson didn't have any family, did he?"

"He never mentioned any," Mike said.

"And Miss Finister?"

"I think she had an apartment near the mobile home park. Lived alone, I guess."

We ran up ahead. The taxi was moving very slowly along that muddy road. As we came close to it, we peered inside.

Dressed in black were two women, one older, one younger, and a girl of about my age.

And sitting on the jump seat, holding the older woman's hand, *was Mr. Bragg*!

12

"Why! Why is he in a family car! Consoling them? He might even be the one who killed Miss Finister! And whoever killed her killed Mr. Emerson also. If he's in there pretending to be kind to the family..."

We trudged through the soft wet earth toward the cemetery gate. The white haze lifted enough for us to see the gravestones. We avoided the path, walking between the stones, which emerged out of the fog like great hulking presences. The wind came whistling between them, not a big wind, just a low sharp whistle that told you that time, like winter, was on its way, and to "be ye also ready."

We saw the group of people around the two open graves. We could see the mourners now, the two women standing together, not crying, just stony-faced. But the girl, who was about my age, she edged away and stood by herself near the now-leafless tree that hung over the yawning holes. I detached myself from Mike's hand. "Detective work."

"Watch yourself," he said.

The girl wore a black dress and a dark pullover. She didn't seem much interested in the funeral. She hugged herself against the cold. She moved over to a stone bench and sat. "Hi," I said. "You here for Miss Finister? Are you related?"

"My great-aunt," she said. "I never really knew her. She left Minnesota before I was old enough. But my mother and grandmother, they always wrote to her."

"I'm Ally McNeil," I said. "I was in Mr. Emerson's class."

"Did he kill her?" she asked. "My mother and grandmother don't think he did. But they won't talk about it much."

"So is your name Finister, too?"

"No. Barog. She was related on my grandmother's side. How can you stand living out here, it's so wet. I only came because she promised me a trip to L.A. afterward. I've never seen Disneyland."

"So if you're related to Miss Finister, why was Mr. Bragg riding with you? Just to show you the way?"

"Bragg?" she said. "Oh, that's my second cousin. His name isn't Bragg, it's Barog. Martin Barog."

In the background I could hear Mr. Foresmith, the minister, giving the usual burial sermon. He only had one. It was written out on a three-by-five card. Every funeral, he just inserted a different name. I knew it by heart. There is a time to live and a time to die, et cetera. I edged over to where Mike stood alone. I saw them lowering the first coffin. "Mike, the girl is with Miss Finister's family from Minnesota. Mr. Bragg's real name is Barog, and he was her second cousin. I just don't get it."

"And look who's standing over there near the stone that looks like a horse." It was a horse. The man who was buried there was a cowboy who asked to be buried with his horse. The stone read: "In the saddle riding into eternity, 1872." Leaning next to the horse was Red Arnold.

"I think we'd better get out of here," Mike said.

We both edged away. Red Arnold was watching us. He shifted a little as he saw us move. I could also see Mr. Bragg standing next to one of the two women. His eyes were not on her as he spoke nor on the grave, but on us. There were also some kids from Mr. Emerson's classes. I saw them huddled together at the edge of the crowd. And standing near them, lighting a cigarette, hunched into his leather jacket with the badge on it, was Marvin Letterman.

We walked slowly away. Luckily the mist caught us and enveloped us. As soon as we were out of sight, we ran. Bits of the town came and went in the white mist. We headed toward the river. Somehow, down in the gully near the water, the white stuff disappeared, like a pocket of clarity. We walked for a long long while, thinking. The whole mystery was just like this, covered in mists with little clearings now and then.

We stopped at our "goose pen" tree. The ground was muddy but the little tree cave was dry.

Mike sat hunched inside his jacket. "Let's go over what we know. Three people here in town had personal reasons for wanting to kill Miss Finister. We also know that somebody from outside hated her: an old Nazi named Franz who never stopped stalking her. But the point of this whole crime is the little black book with the formula. It was the formula they all wanted, and who is the only one here in town who could possibly have known that?"

"Mr. Bragg. He was related to Miss Finister. He might have known!"

"It has to be Bragg. Let's say Miss Finister came to

Martindale to be near Mr. Emerson. For some reason, her nephew followed and got a job here. Everything was fine. She and Mr. Emerson were about to leave town to be happy for what was left of their lives. And then she saw Bragg down by the river."

"And," I said, getting more and more excited, "because river means boy-girl, I've been assuming she saw him with some woman! The one she saw him with was an old German who had come to Martindale looking for a formula that would bring someone a fortune! It was Franz she saw Mr. Bragg talking to down by the river!"

"I think you're right," said Mike. "Franz must have been watching the family back in Minnesota. Maybe he's been hanging around for a long while trying to get to Bragg. Trying to bribe him or something to get the secret out of his aunt. Miss Finister thought she was about to get away. Then one morning she sees her nephew walking down by the river with her most hated enemy. You heard her in the office telling her nephew that she knew the truth. That's why he was so upset."

"And something else!" I said. "I just remembered. When I was in Bragg's office, he had a new blotter on his desk. And I kept looking at that because it was a clue. But I also noticed that he was wearing a Martindale school ring! Your grandfather heard a pinging sound that night he was hit, like a ring hitting the teapot. It could've been Bragg!"

"Bragg and someone else. Red Arnold? But why would someone pretend to be Red Arnold out on the archery court? And what puzzles me most: They wanted that formula. Why kill the only person who could give it to them?"

We heard a creaking of branches. We froze. Someone had followed us. We were trapped there in the goose pen. "Quick," I said, "make a run for it. We may take them by surprise." We moved out of the tree cave ready to make a dash for the river.

Red Arnold stepped in front of us. "Don't move, don't run. I have something to tell you, and if you value your lives, you'd better listen."

13

Mike moved in front of me, which was silly since Red Arnold didn't have a weapon, and I had two kicking feet and two good fists. I slid out from behind Mike and positioned myself.

"Listen to me," Red Arnold warned. "I know that you two found out about Margo and the formula. I was on the porch last night and saw you poking in the ashes. After all these years, burned! If only I could have come a moment sooner. . . ."

"Who are you?" I demanded. "You're not just a maintenance man. Why were you watching Mike's house?"

"Listen, Mike. I've got to get you out of here before they find us. I work with a private agency associated with the U.S. Government. We knew that the German had been tracking Margo all these years. We followed him and found her. We'd been assigned to watch her and try to find out if she still had the formula. If she hadn't fired me that

81

morning, I could have saved her. Now I've got to save you. Mike, the book is gone, but if you can remember any of it that formula—"

Suddenly his eyes lifted. I tried to follow what he'd seen when a hood came down over my head and my arms were pulled roughly behind my back. I heard Mike cry, "Ally, run!" And then his voice was muffled by a hood. My wrists were tied. I was dumped on the ground.

"No!" Red cried. "You can't. Not two children. Think what you're doing! Your whole career, your life, you can't turn against your country this way . . ."

I waited to hear an answer. Nobody else spoke.

". . . you know you can't trust him. You know what he represents. Man, you've fought for your country. You fought against what he believes! Think!"

I heard a small sharp report. A moan. Someone fell to the ground with a heavy thud.

All the while I was working on my hands. I have very small hands. Now, I told you that danger clears my head. When someone started to bind my hands, I held them far apart, as hard as I could. Now I collapsed them. I wriggled my hands, trying to work the ropes loose.

I was working on my hands. I didn't prepare myself for the handkerchief that pressed to the hood right over my nose. Chloroform! Don't breathe, I told myself. I held my breath as long as I could. I tried to tell myself I was swimming underwater, that I had to swim a long long way to the side of the pool. I couldn't make that swim. I took in a breath, and my head began to spin.

I woke up in a dream. I dreamed I was flying with my father. I came to consciousness with the drone of a motor roaring in my ears. I was on the floor. I could feel Mike's body next to mine. He was moving, coming to. The floor was vibrating. *It wasn't a dream! I was on a plane! And we were flying!*

I heard someone say: "They're coming around."

The voice I heard had a faint accent, like someone who had lived a long time in this country but still had a hint of home. He pulled me gruffly into a sitting position. The hood was made of something thin. I could see light through it, nothing more. But I knew that the man who had pulled me so roughly was the man who had hounded poor Margo Von Oster to her death.

14

I felt slightly off balance as the plane made a banking turn. I think the pilot was flying in circles. I kept working on my hands. Now I felt movement as Mike came awake. I was leaning back against what felt like an empty seat. I tried to signal him with my foot that I was all right. I heard Franz's voice, talking to Mike. "We know you found the book with the formula. Where is it? If you value your life, tell us now."

"Burned," said Mike.

I heard a thud. I heard Mike's intake of breath, and then he said, "Hitting me won't change the truth. The formula was written in a diary. I burned it in my fireplace. Look, you'll find the ashes if you don't believe me. I think you know where my fireplace is. You've been there before. You're the bastard who hit my grandfather."

I heard another blow, a hard one, I winced at the force of it. "Now listen, you young brat. Don't be smart with me. The formula was written in a diary, and you read it. You're a smart brat. Maybe you remembered what you read."

One half of me was listening. The other half was squeezing my hands into the smallest possible space and wriggling. The bonds were coming off. It was the listening half of my mind that worried me. By now I knew Mike as well as I knew myself. I'm practical. I do what's necessary to survive. And if lying is necessary, I do it. Not Mike. He was an idealist, a man of honor. He couldn't lie if his life depended on it. And at this moment, his life really depended on it. I tried to project a message into his head. *Don't tell them, Mike! This is not the time for truth! Find a way not to tell them!*

"Yes, I read it. Not only the formula, but the whole story. That's how I know who you are—a Nazi who wanted to enslave the world. Because of men like you, my grandfather is blind."

I felt Franz's foot brush against me as he kicked Mike. "Do you remember anything of the formula?"

Silence. *Mike, don't tell him! Figure out something else to say!*

"You listen to me, brat. I've given up my whole life to find that formula. I've searched for a vile woman who betrayed her country and her cause. Because of her, the whole glorious Nazi dream was crushed to dust. Now the secret is in your hands. I haven't many more years left. The time is now. Do you understand me?" Another kick. But no sound from Mike.

All this time my legs had been free, and now my hands were free. I could have made a move. But we were flying, I didn't know who was at the controls, and I didn't know if Franz had a gun. I couldn't move, not yet.

"I know a quick way, young Lochinvar."

Lochinvar? Who was Lochinvar? I tried to remember

from what lesson we had a Lochinvar, poetry I think, the unit I slept through.

"This girl, I think you like this girl, yes? Let's see how fast you talk. I'm opening the door of the plane, young lover." I felt the wind rush in. Okay. We were in a small plane and flying low, or else we would have been in trouble with altitude and air pressure. The roar of the motors filled the plane, deafening me. Suddenly Franz grabbed me under the arms and began to drag me. I couldn't let him know that my hands were free, it would have cost me the advantage. I could feel him pulling me close to the open door. Wind rushed by me. The roar was deafening. Suddenly my head and shoulders were hanging out in space. "No!" I screamed. I love skydiving. But not without a chute!

"Stop!" Mike shouted. "Don't hurt her! Leave her alone! I'll tell you what you want to know!"

"Tell me now, then I'll pull her in. She's hanging over space, young Romeo. Over empty space."

"No, pull her in and close the door. When I know she's safe."

The door stayed open, but he pulled me back and threw me against Mike so he would know that I was safe. I pressed as close as I could.

"Ally . . ." Mike said. He sounded lost, I could tell that. I wish I could have said to him what my father always said to me: The game isn't over until the fat lady sings. "I read the formula," Mike said. "I have a photographic memory. Let her go and I'll give it to you!"

Franz let out a long and deep and satisfied "ahhhh."

"Close the door!" It was the pilot now. If the roar of the motor hadn't been so loud, I could have heard his voice and known who he was. Franz moved away from us, I suppose to pull the door shut. Suddenly the plane banked very sharply. I slid along the floor, stopped by the side of the plane. I heard Franz shriek "No!" The voice trailed off into space.

I couldn't believe what had happened. *Franz had been dumped! The pilot had banked the plane when Franz was trying to close the door, and Franz had been literally thrown into space!*

Since my hands were free, all I had to do was pull them through the loops of the rope. Suddenly the plane stopped banking. It had leveled off. I couldn't stand it any longer. I had to know what was happening. I pulled off the hood just as the pilot, a chute on his back, stepped from the plane. I jumped to the controls. I looked below. We had been circling the coast, and now we were heading out to sea. It was a small plane, probably a Cessna. I'd flown often enough with my father. I wasn't sure I could land it, but I was pretty sure I could fly it. I made a broad turn and headed back toward the coast.

Below, just beyond the surf, I saw the chute on the water. I was sure he was swimming in to shore.

"What's happening?" Mike screamed. "Ally! Are you there!"

"He bailed out!" I called. "Quick! Make your way over here! I'll untie your hands!" The door was still open, the roar of the motors filling the small plane. Mike edged his way carefully along the floor. I looked below, getting a fix on where we were. I'd already seen the configuration of the coast. My father trained me in land configurations. He knew I'd want to pilot my own plane one day. I recognized the little inlet near Grayland Beach. We were less than thirty miles from home.

Mike slithered across the floor until he found me. We were headed northeast. I reached down and pulled off his hood. I managed to get the rope knots with one hand. Now Mike was free. He sat there, rubbing his hands, trying to understand what had happened. "Quick," I said, "find the chutes. We're flying low. I can make out the freeway down there. We're headed as close as I can figure back toward Martindale, but I don't think I can land this plane, so we'll have to jump for it."

Mike's eyes showed how he felt. I tried to keep the plane level as he crawled to the storage locker. He began to search for chutes. We'd already passed Aberdeen. I thought if I could see the thick stand of trees to the east of the town, if I could spot the church steeple, or if I could just follow the river...

And then I saw real trouble. The gas gauge. Empty!

Mike was back at my side. "Ally, there's only one parachute."

Okay. My head was clear. I searched for landmarks. We'd passed the old dam west of the town. I knew where we were. "We get as close to the town as we can manage, and then we jump."

Mike bent close to me. "Did you hear what I said? There's only one chute. Ally, put it on. Quick." His arms were around me. He bent his head to mine. *Mike Sloane kissed me!*

It was meant as a good-bye.

The motor began to sputter.

I put the plane on automatic. "Quick. Don't argue. One chance. I'll flatten myself against you. Tie the chute around both of us and when we fall, wrap your legs around me and hang on! I'll hold as tight as I can. Don't think! Act now!"

He acted. I hugged against him. He strapped the chute onto both of us, putting the buckles around my back. I reached over and got hold of the ripcord. "Tell me when!" he shouted against the roar of the motor. I knew he was panicked. "Tell me how!" I couldn't tell him anything. We were starting down. If the angle were wrong, we might get hit by the wings of the plane. Before he could say anything else, I maneuvered him to the open door and leaned out. I heard him scream. We hadn't made a good start, and so we began to tumble in free-fall. His arms and legs were glued around me. It was pretty hairy. I pulled the cord. The ground was coming up pretty fast. Suddenly a hard jerk and we were pulled up straight.

The worst was over! I told you I loved to jump. It's a dangerous sport, and I was forbidden until I was old enough to make up my own mind. But right now we were safe! We'd survived! And this was the beautiful part! Floating in open space, Mike's arms around me, swinging through the pristine sky. Well, not exactly pristine. It was pretty hazy. But I felt safe enough to remember that Mike had offered me his life. One chute, and he gave it to me. And that kiss. Not only that, he would have given the formula, which was his honor, to save my life.

I looked below. I saw a lovely wheat field and behind that a barn and a haystack. If we could only land in that! Then we'd find ourselves in each other's arms, and he could repeat that kiss. We were still in a rather precarious position, but all I could think of was rainbows.

The haystack came and went. We moved over the barn toward a pig wallow, a little mud pond with about three pigs squishing in it.

Yuk!

We hit, tumbled over and over in the yuk mud. I tried to unfasten the lines but they were mud-stuck. I had a mouth full of pig mud. Blechhh! "Loosen the lines!" I called. Mike didn't know how. He rose and slipped. Finally I was able to roll away. Slosh. Squish. Three pigs stood watching us.

And then a farmer with a shotgun came running out of the barn. "You weekend jumpers, if I see one more of you on my place, it's buckshot, do you hear me! Now get the blazes off my land!"

Try running with mud in your shoes, in your hair, in your clothes, not just mud, but I can't describe what manner of mud.

But we were safe, alive. Somehow the mud deadened our sense of renewal. I was spitting mud out of my mouth. Mike was pulling mud out of his hair. We were a couple of miles from the fork, Puddleston one way, Martindale the other. And we had things to say, things to do with love and survival, thanks and celebration. But we were two people encased in mud. And now the excitement was beginning to wear off. I felt so yukky I thought I would die if I didn't have an immediate shower. But we had something to say! This was probably the most important moment of our lives. "Mike, I—"

But he must have been in shock, to find himself in a plane, threatened with death, his honor at stake as well as his life, and jumping and all that. And the landing. Well, if you'd never jumped, you can imagine. It was all just wearing off. He looked, as best I could see his expression when he was encased in sticky goo, like a man about to explode. Something formed in him, something big, swelling. "Why—" he began, sputtering to get gook out from his mouth, "why didn't you warn me before we jumped!"

He probably almost died of fright.

We had loving things to say, important things, but he was exploding, and I was furious. I mean, I saved his life with my fast thinking! If we hadn't jumped then . . .

We came to the fork, stood there for a moment, two clay figures, pieces of mud falling off, my hair full of other stuff, I won't dare to describe it. He went one way, I went the other.

I trudged gookily all the way home.

I got home to an empty house. I dumped my yuk shoes in the trash, my good Reeboks. I washed the first layer off me with the hose. Then, wrapped in an old garage blanket, trying not to drip, I dumped my clothes in the laundry and got into the shower and stood there until the pig yuk washed down into the drain. Three washings of my hair and I still felt icky. I cleaned under my fingernails, washed out my mouth. I could still taste it.

I heard the front door slam. Orville came running upstairs. "Where were you! You told Mom you'd be home right after the funeral! She's out playing tennis and I was all alone!"

Only now was it beginning to dawn on me that I had faced almost certain death. Suddenly I wanted Mom and I wanted Daddy to come home. I even wanted Orville. I hugged him, I actually hugged him. He pushed me away, very suspicious.

"Orville," I said, "you won't believe what happened to me. I was kidnapped, chloroformed, taken up in a plane, my life threatened, the pilot bailed out leaving us with a plane without gas, Mike and I had to jump with only one chute between us and we landed in a pigsty."

He gave me this big punch to the shoulder. "Thanks a lot for nothing. I don't need your stupid lies, okay!"

By the time I got into bed, I was really shaky. I was still free-falling. First it was the shock of Red Arnold's revelation and the chloroform and the death threat in the air, and then the escape and the disappointment of my final moments with Mike. And suddenly now I was back being sixteen in my own room with the ruffled curtains my mom and I had made, and my stuffed bear sitting on the pillow beside me. The phone rang.

It had to be Mike. I picked it up. This wasn't danger, it was love and infinitely more scary. He had come to himself and realized what had happened, and he wanted to apologize, and I knew Mike Sloane, he'd be too embarrassed to say it. I had to say it, now. "I love you, okay? We could have died out there, and you never would have known. I want you to know now."

"I love you, too," said Francine's voice. "And don't die yet. Do you remember that Monday is the junior class picnic? I guess you and Mike are hot and heavy, but we're off on Monday for Olympia to see the salmon run."

15

I still wasn't taking it in.

"The picnic? Tour of the brewery? Lunch near the salmon ladder? Walk to the Deschutes River to see the salmon run? You were on the committee! So, what's happening between you and Mike?"

"Forget it. Please forget I said it, okay?"

"Sure. Absolutely. Forgotten. Are you going steady with him? Did he give you a ring or a locket or anything?"

"If we're still going on the picnic, who's the sponsor? Mr. Nightengale is gone. Who's taking us up to Olympia?"

"Who do you think? Mr. Bragg."

Now I was home in my own bed. Now I wasn't a sky-jumper who loved floating through space. I was just Ally McNeil, about three years old, wishing her father would get back from flying around the world.

"You okay?" Francine asked.

"Sure, just tired I guess. I think I'll stay in tomorrow,

93

catch up on my homework. So I'll see you on Monday morning."

I pulled the covers up over my head. I was on overload.

When the phone rang again, I wasn't in the mood for any more Francine. I picked it up and said, "Please, I'll explain Monday morning, okay, Francine? I'd like to get some rest today." I heard silence, and breathing. It wasn't Francine. "Mike? Is that you?"

His voice seemed choked up. He was searching for words. "You . . . you saved my life, Ally. I won't ever forget what you did up there. . . ."

"What *you* did. You offered me the only chute."

"Ally . . . I . . ."

Please say it. *I love you, Ally.* It's not hard. Just open your mouth, and let it out.

He couldn't. He was speechless. Because affairs of the heart aren't logical. He must have been way off his foundation, mixed up by his feelings. "The reason I didn't phone sooner," he said, "was that I went back to the goose pen to look for Red Arnold. There was blood on the ground and on the leaves. Someone dragged him away."

"And Franz is out at sea. And the plane came down in the high trees."

"Did you see the pilot?"

"He'd already jumped. All I saw was his back."

"Could you hear his voice?"

"Too much motor noise. But it's got to be Bragg! Who else is left?"

"I agree," Mike said. "I think it was Bragg."

"Then we've really got ourselves a problem," I said. "Because if he was the pilot, he thinks we're dead. And we're not. We're still in Martindale."

"And so is he," said Mike.

"Worse than that. Monday is the junior class picnic. Guess who's going to guide us through the brewery and over the bridge to see salmon swimming upstream?"

I heard the intake of breath. "Mr. Bragg."

"So what do we do?"

"*We* do nothing. *I* do," Mike said. "You've done enough. That chute might not have held the two of us. You risked your life for me."

"Forget it. Nothing is going to keep me away from the finish," I said.

"No. This time it's my turn. I go on the picnic, I find a way to corner him and get him to make an admission. I have to hear him say it. Only then will I know that Mr. Emerson and his sad life will be avenged."

"You and me. Ally and Mike. We're partners until this crime is solved. Remember? And if you go back on that, it's a breach of contract or honor or something. So I'll wait for you in front of the school. The bus leaves at nine. As far as Bragg knows, we're dead, and he's waiting now for news that two Martindale students are missing. If he doesn't hear anything, if he walks out there on Monday and sees us waiting for the bus, we'll know, won't we? So I'll see you Monday."

Another silence. "Ally. . ."

I waited. *Please . . . now . . . just say it.*

He couldn't. "See you Monday," he said.

I lay there dreaming of all the things he could have said, and things I could have answered.

I heard the door open. And I heard the door shut.

My mother stood there holding this pukey pair of jeans, this yukked-up article of clothing. "Something smelled funny on my way past the laundry. All right, what's the story?"

16

What's the story?

The story was the story, but it just wasn't as simple as that.

I looked at my problem in the logical way.

First of all, she was my mother, and I owed her the truth.

On the other hand, I had told Orville the truth and look what happened. If I told her that I'd been chloroformed and almost dumped out of a plane, she'd die of upset. She'd be all off balance, half deliriously happy that I wasn't dead, half furious that I'd gotten myself into that mess. And the danger was past, so what was the purpose of stirring it up? And then, she might not even believe me.

On the other hand, I had to tell her something.

"Do you trust me?"

Mothers, good mothers, are supposed to say "Of course, darling, I'll always trust you." But she was pretty cool to kids, if you know what I mean. "In what context?" she said. "Trust you in what context? Trust you with drugs or with the car? Of course. You've got a head on you. You wouldn't smoke, you wouldn't drink, you drive carefully. But if you mean with some of your other stunts . . ."

Stunts? What other stunts? I never tried any stunts I didn't think I could handle! Did she mean the free-fall dive that time when she didn't know I was going? That time we were learning how to join up in the shape of a star during the fall, and I just managed to miss my hand-partner, and I kept falling for a long long time, forgetting to pull the cord? Did she mean that? That wasn't a stunt, that was a learning process. And I'd promised never to do it again! "Look," I said, "I've decided what I'm going to do with my life. I'm not going to be just a silly, aimless girl."

"When, tell me when, were you ever that! When you were fifteen months old, you climbed to the upper bunk of your bed, you remember that bunk bed? And you stood there waiting for someone, yelling 'catch me!' Allison, what are you into!"

Tell her something. You owe that to your mother. "Okay. I've been investigating the crime. After all, they killed someone very close to me."

"Miss Finister was close?"

"Mr. Emerson was close."

"Mr. Emerson killed himself! He was probably guilty, and he couldn't stand the pressure."

"Mom, trust me. Mr. Emerson died of a broken heart. I can't tell you why, not now. And the man who murdered Miss Finister is still at large. We think, Mike and I think, we know who it is, and on Monday we'll know for sure. Monday it will be all over, and Mr. Emerson will be avenged. So please just trust me until then."

"Monday where?"

"We're going up to Olympia on a junior class picnic to see the salmon going upstream."

"You're going to find a murderer on a salmon run?"

"Yes, I think so."

She held up the odorous jeans. "What about these?"

Remembering the "stunt" with the free-fall diving, I avoided that part of it. "I fell into a pig wallow."

"How!"

How. "Mike and I were looking for clues—"

"In a barnyard?"

I was floundering for an answer.

"Never mind," she said. "Forget it. I wash my hands of it. Your father will be home Monday night. Let him handle it. Monday you're going to a class picnic, and you expect to find a murderer among the salmon going up to spawn. Great. Inspires great trust, that story. Just rest assured that you won't be going on a murderer-hunting picnic unchaperoned."

What did she mean? Was she coming along on the picnic? She couldn't! You can't go murderer-hunting with your partner who also happened to be someone just on the verge of admitting his great love, et cetera, with your mother along!

So on Sunday I got very industrious. I stayed in my room, doing all my back homework. My mother looked in a couple of times with that curious expression. Homework on Sunday?

I didn't watch TV on Sunday night, not even *Murder, She Wrote*, which I always loved. Even Orville popped into my room, giving me bizarre little looks.

I was up early on Monday morning. I showered, packed myself a lunch so that I'd have plenty of time to talk my mother out of this "chaperoning" thing. Orville left for school early—he liked to play kickball before class. My mother was just putting away the breakfast stuff, her robe still on. She didn't look as if she were coming along. Should I say something? I decided to let well enough alone. "So I'm going now."

"Have a good time," she said. She was not particularly smiling. She didn't like these long single spaces when my father was away. She was great in her business, on planes, in sports, but she frazzled out with long stretches of kids.

I left quickly.

Francine was waiting outside. "What happened? Is he in love with you, too? Did he actually say so in so many words? Please tell me, I'm dying to hear."

"I hope that by tonight I can tell you everything."

I heard the snort and roar of a motorcycle. Garth Meacham skidded to a stop. "Been looking everywhere for you. Got a minute?"

Francine was still uncomfortable with him. She backed away a little. But I liked Garth, I couldn't help myself. "Sure. What's up?"

"Got accepted to forestry school."

"That's wonderful! I'm really happy for you. We'll celebrate at the picnic today."

He balanced on his motorcycle. "You going to that stupid thing?"

I looked around to make sure we weren't being overheard. Francine had walked away a bit but was trying to hear. "Listen, some really dramatic things have happened. And Mike and I think we know who committed the murder, so you'll be relieved to know you'll be absolutely in the clear. We'll find out today at the picnic."

Garth gave me the oddest glance. I couldn't really work out in my head what his eyes were saying. "Look, watch yourself," he said. "You've been really good to me. I won't forget it. I don't want to see you get hurt." And he gunned his cycle and drove off.

As I saw him leave I had this prickly feeling at the back

of my neck. Stupid. Dummy. You're trying to keep all of this to yourself. Why on earth did you tell Garth!

Francine came to walk beside me. "You're getting pretty chummy with Garth," she said. "I heard that he's dropping out of school." She walked ahead so that she could turn and see my face. "Ally, are you okay?"

"Not okay," I said. "I know how caterpillars feel when they get into a cocoon and then wait for the transformation. I'm trying to learn to be logical. It's not easy. I hope I haven't spoiled anything."

"What do you mean, anything?"

"I can't tell you yet."

She was trying to catch my eye. I was walking head down to avoid her. "You're making me really nervous. Ally, I swear, I've been in total abstinence for four... okay, for three days. Don't tempt me to eat my lunch before twelve o'clock."

"I'm proud of you," I said. "I'll just tell you this. If things go as I think they're going to go, you'll see the biggest scandal Martindale has had since the president of Martindale Savings ran off to St. Louis with his wife's sister."

We could see kids milling around the lawn as we entered the school grounds. There, parked just inside, was a police car.

And sitting in the car was Marvin Letterman!

He waved me over. He was laughing at something. "I heard you and Mike are off to do a little hunting." Amusement played at the corners of his mouth.

"What do you mean 'hunting'? We're going to see the fish go upstream. We don't try to catch them. They're spawning."

He grinned. "No, I mean murderer-hunting. Your mother called this morning. I told her it was a kid stunt.

She said that there were too many funny things going on in
Martindale, and she demanded that we keep an eye on you
two. So I'm on special assignment to chaperone the junior
class picnic." He laughed that high-pitched laugh of his.
"Maybe you'll find a killer salmon!"

Francine was absolutely having kittens. "What is he
talking about!"

"I'll tell you tonight." I searched for Mike. The bus was
pulling up. The kids were already lining up to get aboard.
First period sounded. The big oak double doors of the
school were usually closed after first-period bell to trap
latecomers around to the side gate, where they got zapped.
Now the big doors opened.

Mr. Bragg walked out.

Mike came flying around the corner, leaning into his
handlebars. He pumped his bike to where I stood, hit the
brakes, jumped off. "Look," I said.

His eyes followed mine. Mr. Bragg had started across
the grass toward the bus.

I took Mike's hand. He pressed mine. Mr. Bragg
walked head bent, face clouded, really upset. We ran for
the bus and lined up with the rest.

Mr. Bragg looked terrible, really broken. He walked
past the kids in line and climbed on the bus. He saw us! He
had to see us standing there, but his face registered nothing! He wasn't himself, he seemed upset, a little distracted,
there was a look in his eyes of something, but not shock!

I was the one who was shocked. I looked to Mike. He
stared after Mr. Bragg with puzzled eyes.

And then Marvin Letterman, in his police jacket,
climbed on board. As he passed me, he leaned down and
whispered. "Maybe a salmon chewed her to death." He
was still laughing as he fell into the seat beside Mr. Bragg.

We started to roll. Everyone settled down for the ride. I
sat at the window, Mike beside me. Francine sat behind us,

poking at me, trying to get my attention. My attention was on Mr. Bragg.

The whole drive was only a half hour. The kids started to sing "Row, Row, Row Your Boat." Marvin Letterman's voice, which was really pretty good, boomed out with the rest. He was having a good time. It was just a fun outing to see the salmon run. A tour of the brewery, a walk through the neat gardens, a chance to see the salmon ladders, and then a hike through town to the Deschutes River, where you can really see salmon. I voted for the trip. They've had some bad salmon years up this way. Too much sport fishing, with everybody wanting to eat fish to avoid cholesterol and all that, and the Indians making a point that the fishing belonged to them. The salmon population had been running thin. But this year the fish were spectacular.

I wasn't thinking of salmon. I was thinking of murder!

It had to be Bragg! He was the only one who could have known! His aunt saw him *down by the river*! That had to have been him and Franz! So why didn't he look shocked when he saw us?

Because he was a master actor. Because he cold-bloodedly killed his aunt and clobbered Mike's grandfather and shot a government agent who was probably his friend and swung an airplane around so that his partner in crime fell out of it. So he saw us. Of course he wouldn't register. He just put on an act. Heartbroken nephew, so upset that his aunt had been murdered by a crazy old man.

We bumped along toward Olympia. They were singing the school song, "Martindale Forever."

Suddenly I heard the sound of cycles. The Devils roared by, Garth among them. He turned to the bus as he passed it. He saw me, waved, leaned into the wind, and sped on. So Garth had decided to come after all. I felt a little prickling at the back of my neck. *Why?*

We pulled into the brewery parking lot. Bragg swung

off the bus. He had the list in his hand. He was checking us off, one by one. "This is it," said Mike. "Let me go first."

We waited until the end of the line. Only Marvin Letterman was behind us. He poked me. "Something fishy going on?" He laughed.

To tell you the truth, I was glad he was there just in case something happened.

Mike stepped off the bus. "Michael Sloane," said Mr. Bragg in a clear voice. I thought I saw his hand shake a bit. Nothing else. He checked Mike off.

I stepped off the bus. "Allison McNeil," I said. "What was it Miss Finister saw down by the river?"

Now I saw shock! He dropped the list, fumbled to pick it up. He tried to speak, but his mouth had a funny shape. *We had him!* He turned and ran after the group that was headed toward the brewery for the tour. We saw him enter the building. "What are you guys up to?" Marvin asked.

We didn't answer. Mike tried to hold me back as he rushed after Mr. Bragg. I wouldn't be held back. I wanted to be in at the finish.

17

We started the tour in the trophy room. There were hundreds of decorated beer steins, royal steins, famous steins. We weren't interested in steins. We were interested in justice.

We moved to the ingredients room where a really nice guide named Fred Metcalfe showed us how beer was brewed. Ordinarily I wouldn't really care how beer was made but now I was being logical, looking for details, thinking with clarity. They take malt and barley, which they cook in a mash tub. Then they cook corn, which lightens the taste. Then they mix corn and malt, which gets converted to sugar. And then they strain the whole mess out in a lauter tub, like a big strainer. The juice is called wort. They put the wort in an enormous kettle and add the hops for spice. Then the whole goopy mess is strained and the yeast is added, and it goes into cold vats to age. And if you think all that was easy to hang on to while my heart and mind and eyes were on Mr. Bragg, well, becoming a detective wasn't easy. We moved along a very cold hall. We zipped up jackets or pulled on sweaters.

Fred Metcalfe was telling us how beer had been brewed ever since there had been agriculture but it was the Germans who probably added the hops.

German. Franz came back to me, his voice on the plane, that scream as he dropped off into space.

Mr. Bragg fell back behind the group. Mike and I both saw it. Something was wrong. Mr. Bragg seemed crushed, as if something awful were weighing him down. I could see tears in his eyes.

Finally. He'd cracked. "This is it," I said. The tour moved on toward the great room with its enormous vats. Mike and I had waited for that moment. We walked over to where Bragg stood, crushed, beaten, in tears. "I think you might as well admit it all," Mike said. "We're here. We're not floating in the Pacific. And there are people all around us. Even the police are here. It's too late to hide the truth. We know that Miss Finister was Margo Von Oster. We also know that she was your aunt. Ally heard her say she'd seen you down by the river. We know the German was there. You might as well admit it all."

He uttered a little sob. "I killed her," he said.

So that was it. The truth was known. It was over.

"I killed her"—he sobbed—"as surely as if I'd done it myself. She was my great-aunt. She was always good to me. She knew I hated it there on the farm. She sent me money to go to college. She even helped me to get the job teaching in Martindale. I knew the whole story, you see. My grandmother knew it, and she'd told me before I left for Washington. She wanted me to keep an eye on my aunt. But I wasn't satisfied. I wanted more. I wanted to get down to California, get myself a really nice car..." He looked to Mike and me as if he wanted somebody to understand. "And then when the German came to see me . . ."

"Franz," said Mike.

"The German from the chemical company. He said that the formula was worth millions, and that my aunt's case was officially closed years ago, and that if I'd only talk her out of the formula, there would be millions for her, and for me. She could go away with Emerson. They could get married. Why not sell the formula now?

"But I thought about it. I would never do anything without asking her. I intended to talk to her that night. But she'd seen us down by the river. Suddenly I realized that he'd tricked me. She must have thought I betrayed her. What would my family think? I had to make her understand.

"It was right after you left, Ally. I went into the office. I saw the storeroom door open. She was dead. I was in a panic. Had the German killed her for the formula? She wouldn't have had it with her! It was crazy! I ran back to my office, to try to think what to do. Meanwhile, Emerson came in and found her. They accused him of the murder, and he didn't protest. He couldn't, without telling their secret." He put his hands up to his face. "And I let him do it. I was too frightened to tell the truth. It would mean my job, everything. I don't know who did it. I only know it was my fault. I killed her as much as if I'd put my hands around her neck."

Mike and I stood there watching a shattered man, but he *wasn't the man on the plane! He wasn't the man who had hit Mike's grandfather! And he wasn't the man who had killed Miss Finister!*

"Will you two hurry!" called Marvin Letterman. "I don't want you falling behind! It's bad enough to be stuck baby-sitting a bunch of kids. Don't make it any harder by splitting the group!"

I had to poke Mike to get him going. He was standing there, running through his shattered logic, really mixed up.

So was I. It wasn't Bragg. Who was left? Red Arnold was gone. Mr. Bragg was a rat, not a murderer.

Marvin Letterman was waiting impatiently for us. He looked down. His shoelace was untied. He lifted his foot to tie it, setting his boot on a metal rail. The cleats on the bottom made a pinging sound.

Mike heard it and I heard it.

And then I remembered that day we'd met him in the courthouse, the musical way he walked with those cleats on his shoes. *Ping*, the shoe went again. A ringing sound, Mike's grandfather said, like metal against metal. Like the metal cleat of a shoe kicking metal.

Ping.

We waited until Marvin Letterman stood up, his shoe tightly tied. We walked over to where he waited. What Mike said he said slowly and clearly. "I have the whole formula in my head. And you've been paid to make sure nobody ever finds that formula. So what are you going to do about it?"

Marvin Letterman stretched. He took off his cap, flicked something off his visor, and put it on again. "You interested in that next part of the tour? Or would you like to take a walk down by the river and watch salmon going upstream? I think we'd better talk."

He and Mike started out of the brewery.

Marvin Letterman waited at the door for me. He let me pass through. "Ladies first," he said.

His voice went through me like a knife. None of the silly, high-pitched, half-joking way he talked. His voice was lower, colder. As I moved along, he put a hand to my shoulder, as if to guide me.

I knew that hand.

At least I thought I did.

I could have been wrong! What I needed was absolute truth! Be logical. Marvin Letterman didn't say anything but *Let's take a walk.* He could have meant *You two are really acting bizarre, let's get out of here and talk it over.* Maybe his voice wasn't really lower. Maybe it was just me.

It was a short walk to the Deschutes River. You could get a good view of the salmon from the bridge.

We had just turned onto the main road when out of the corner of my eye, I saw Garth Meacham.

When I turned again, he was gone.

18

We walked through town like three warm friends, Marvin's arms around Mike's shoulder and mine. He was shorter then Mike, thinner, but there was a lot of bounce to him. I could tell he had an athlete's body by the way he walked. I'd never noticed that before. But I'd never had to, had I? We walked at a good stride, his cleated boots making a ringing sound on the concrete of the road.

"Pretty smart, the two of you. That's what Captain Mitchell said when he told me to keep an eye on you. Martindale's finest. Pretty girl, going to be just like her mother. Father a pilot," he said.

"That's right."

"You can pilot a plane, they tell me. And pretty feisty. You know what Captain Mitchell told me this morning? To warn me to keep a good keen eye on you? That you'd sky-jumped without permission. Daredevil, he said."

"Daredevil means that I take unnecessary chances. I don't do that anymore."

I still wasn't sure. Neither was Mike. He kept close to Marvin as he walked, listening hard, trying to be absolutely certain.

"And you, you're top of your class. They tell me you actually have a photographic memory." The bridge was in sight. The street was empty. Marvin scanned the street. "Everybody's at lunch. I guess we'll have the bridge to ourselves."

Mike's eyes told the whole story. *He had said nothing about a photographic memory except to the man who tried to push me out of the plane.*

The river wasn't too wide at this point. You could easily swim from one side to the other, and we could see even before we walked onto the bridge that the water was churning. "Would you look at that sight," Marvin said. "I've always meant to come up here to see the salmon run, but I've never had the time. Look at that mess of fish! Unbelievable."

He looked over the bridge railing. So did I. I watched the humped backs of the salmon on the last great effort of a long journey. And it was true what he'd said. I'd seen fish, hundreds of them, going up this piece of the river. But this was spectacular; there were thousands of them, almost bank to bank, some of them leaping out of the water, a moving, living mass working upstream against the current.

"Bright boy," he said to Mike. "You could have had a brilliant career. I heard you were up for a scholarship to Harvard. I went to Harvard, did you know that?"

Mike straightened up slowly. "What would a Harvard man be doing on the Martindale police force? We were told you went up to Seattle every week to study law part-time."

"Well, I like the climate. And the sports, actually. I'm quite a sportsman." He flexed his shoulders as I'd seen him

do before. "I like to climb, I'm a crackerjack swimmer..."
His eyes were down at the stream. "I'm also a crack shot."

"And an archer," said Mike.

Marvin smiled, showing split front teeth. Marvin with
his high giggle and his rather dumb ways was always sort
of a joke to me. I could see now that *he* was the actor. He
wasn't making jokes now. His voice was low-pitched. He
was dead serious. "Archery is an ancient art. I always
loved reading about medieval times. They understood the
use of power even more than we do. Oh, yes, I'm a fine
archer. And law isn't what I study in Seattle. I had reports
to file. I happen to be a lawyer. Not a very good one. If
you don't make top of your class, you can't really hope for
the big money."

"And money is what you wanted," said Mike.

Marvin was bending over the rail, watching this unbelievable spectacle of fish pushing against the current, leaping up, wriggling up. "Money can buy a lot of things. No,
law wasn't what I wanted. So I found myself a better job."

"So you came here to work for the government," I said.
"You fought for our country once."

"Vietnam. I'm a good combat soldier." He grinned with
sly satisfaction. "Wouldn't think of it to look at me. I was
decorated twice."

"So was my grandfather," said Mike. "Decorated for
bravery. You fought for your country and then betrayed it."

Marvin shrugged. "It's a job of work, Mike. One company offered me a salary, another company offered me
more money than I could ever spend. What was I to do?
The people who hired me wanted the formula destroyed. I
had to destroy it. Just a job of work.

"Red Arnold and I were trying to locate the formula.
Then Franz came along. I used Franz, who tried to get the
formula through that idiot Bragg. Red thought I was working with Franz. No. I was working for myself. But Franz

went out of control. He'd been searching for Margo, who had cost him his army commission and his honor. He bribed the stationery delivery man to let him make the delivery that day, and he went mad when he saw her. He strangled her."

I was furious. "But they said that the delivery man was innocent!"

He smiled. "*I* said. That was the story I told. Who would question the police on a thing like that?"

"So it was you," said Mike, "who tried to kill me at the archery stacks."

Marvin laughed. He was enjoying this. "I had no intention of killing you. I assure you that if I had, the arrow would have hit its mark. No. You two were so curious. I had to smoke out the formula, and I knew you'd do it for me. So I simply made you more curious. It brought you to Emerson and to the book."

"But somebody is bound to find Red Arnold's body," I said.

He leaned over the rail, watching the salmon jump and twist in the water. "They'll find a burned car of an alcoholic who drank and drove."

"And the plane. It came down in the trees."

"It should have gone into the ocean. But there's lush foliage in this wet climate. Winter will come, and the rain and the vines will grow over it. I told you, it's a job, and I'm good at my job."

"And us," I said. Now I was primed and ready. I moved slightly away from him so that I could get a good kick. I saw the bulge of his gun holster under his jacket. But how could he shoot us? If they found bodies with bullets in them, he'd be suspected. He'd left the brewery with us. Somebody must have noticed. There was no way he could hurt us here.

He leaned over to look at the flow of moving fish.

"Where do these salmon come from anyway?"

My eyes were glued to him, waiting. "Up from Puget Sound. They spill over into the freshwater lake and then they swim upstream here toward the brewery and spawn up there where they have the fish hatcheries."

Marvin leaned over the railing. "I don't think anyone could swim through that. There isn't an inch of water. I suppose they'd just suck you under."

I never had a chance to digest what he'd said. He had me by the waist. He was stronger than I realized. He flipped me over the rail.

I was falling! I didn't have time to scream! I hit water as I'd never hit water before. I'm a strong swimmer, but this was crazy. I hit a slithery, moving mass. I was pulled under. In a moment Mike hit the water beside me. He must have jumped in.

Now all of this I figured out later. Marvin Letterman was in a crunch. In his head he must have figured, he'd throw me in, Mike would jump in after me, the current would catch us. But we might have been good swimmers, and so he leaped over the rail, too. I think what was in his mind was that he'd grab onto us and hold us under until we drowned and then claim we pulled some kid stunt—well, you know Ally McNeil, the sky-jumping fool. He'd tried to save us, but we drowned. He'd be the hero, not the villain.

But what Marvin didn't know was that the river was only waist deep at that point. And that although the wild churning rush of salmon prevented us from getting our footing, there was hardly a way for him to hold us under water. He was a strong swimmer, I could tell that. He caught hold of my sweater, trying to pull me down. The fish were slimy and slithery. He couldn't get a hand grasp. Mike tried to catch Marvin's jacket. Marvin got a hold on Mike's neck and tried to pull him under. He couldn't. Marvin was probably a clever Harvard man and a strong combat soldier, but he didn't know doodley about North Coast rivers and salmon pushing their way upstream trying to spawn. I had a momentary glimpse of him as I got a brief footing. He'd lost his hold on Mike. He was surrounded by fish, bewildered by fish.

Suddenly a rope flew over my head and was pulled taut! I saw Garth on the bank of the river. I caught the rope. Another Devil stood on the opposite bank! "Mike!" He saw the rope, managed to catch it. We were able to walk hand over hand, salmon battering against us. Half sliding, soaked and fish-grimy, we reached the shore.

Only then did we see Marvin Letterman struggling with the river. He must have been shocked to see Garth. He was still trying to get his footing, the river rushing down, the leaping salmon pushing up. And then he stumbled. His head cracked against the cement post that held up the bridge. He went down!

Mike ran for the rope that rested on the muddy shore. He tied it about his waist. Even then, even after everything, he couldn't see a man drown. But in the midst of those churning fish, we saw Marvin Letterman's hand. He must have been weighted down by his boots and by his gun and jacket. The water was carrying him downstream against the mass of fish. Mike started into the river, but it was too late. We saw Marvin bob up once, pushed by the force of the salmon determined to finish the last few miles of their struggle for the survival of their species. And then he went down.

"Gone," Garth said. "I could hardly believe it when I saw him trying to dump you into the river. What is this all about anyway?"

"If you hadn't been there . . . But what," I asked, "were you doing there?"

"You said you were going to the picnic, and you had

some sort of crazy scheme going on. You've been a good friend to me, Ally. I had the guys drive up to Olympia with me. I never had you out of my sight."

They found the body late that evening, almost down to Columbia Lake, floating in some reeds. The salmon had accomplished their mission. He'd only got what he deserved. Justice.

19

Now, Mike is an honorable man. Truth is truth. But there was no way we could tell the truth this time. So this is the story we told:

Marvin Letterman had wanted to see the salmon. We went down with him. He'd come from the east, he wasn't really a "local," he was trying to get a good look. He'd leaned over too far and lost his footing and slipped in. We tried our best to save him, in fact they tried to make heroes of us, but poor Marvin drowned.

Garth and the Devils corroborated our story. Of course, they'd seen Marvin dump me in. They didn't understand why we tried to protect him. But as a favor to Garth, they let it ride.

Why, you ask, didn't we want the world to know the real truth about the Margo-Emerson affair? About Marvin Letterman and Red Arnold and sad, weak Mr. Bragg?

It was the formula, tucked safely inside of Mike's head.

So that when he's older and wiser, when he knows what's really good for mankind, he'll be able to decide what to do with it. If we'd told all, they'd know about the formula, and the struggle for it, the stupid killing would go on.

Mike and I were taken back to my house. Captain Mitchell, who drove in from Martindale, brought us home himself, lamenting that it was a terrible accident, a terrible loss. He had been going to retire and give Marvin the job. "A Harvard man," said Captain Mitchell, "came to me with a sterling record. Could have done much better. Been in government service, in fact. But he wanted to live up here in Martindale, do some studying. He was a sportsman, did you know that? Crack shot. Poor man, going under like that, dying under fish."

Nobody was home. Mom was off to Seattle with Orville to pick Daddy up. I got out of my fish clothes, into a robe. Mike showered. I gave him some of Daddy's things.

I made us a cup of cocoa. We were alone there in the warm and cozy kitchen. Suddenly it was all over. "They'll always believe Mr. Emerson guilty," said Mike. "But I can't really undo that, at least not now."

"We know he was innocent. We know that the two of them are lying side by side, finally, for eternity."

It was just Mike and me now, sipping our cocoa. He in Daddy's jeans—he wasn't quite as tall as Daddy, so he'd turned up the cuffs—me in my really prettiest robe, my hair brushed out, looking as "adorable" (honestly I hate that word, but at the moment it was important that I look as good as I possibly could, since I'd never have a moment like this one again) as I could. "So, I guess we did it."

He swallowed hard before he said, "I guess we did." And the way he looked at me when he said it was the way I'd been praying he'd look at me from the first. "Ally..." he began. *Okay. Go slow but say it now, please!* "Ally... you're the most extraordinary... I love the way you have the nerve to jump into things. It's not only . . . not just courage . . . it's a way you have of . . ." *Yes, say it. Tell me how I stuck by you and cared about you and how much your grandpa likes me and how you and I would be so good together, . . . say it, Mike! Now!*

He put down his cup. There was perspiration on his forehead. His hands moved slowly to my shoulders. They rested there for a moment. He moved closer, closer, he closed his eyes, I closed my eyes . . .

I heard the door burst open. "Ally, Daddy's—"

Orville was about to say "Daddy's home" when he saw the two of us. Mike had already jumped away, probably so traumatized that he'd never try to kiss me again. He stood, drowning in embarrassment.

Not any more than Awful McNeil who had seen exactly what he'd done. "Uh-oh." He backed away. In his eyes was total fear. He knew what I was going to do to him.

And then Mom and Daddy stepped in. They'd been through town, they'd stopped at the market for a few things, they'd already heard. Daddy gave me such a hug. And then Daddy shook Mike's hand. Proud to meet him. Mike looked as if he wanted to crawl away and die somewhere. The first moment he could, he said he really had to go home to his grandfather. Daddy and Mom said they'd drive him, they wouldn't think of letting him go back on his own. Daddy said he was just thankful that . . . well, he'd hear the whole story when he got back from Puddleston.

Mom looked at me, half concerned, half puzzled, not knowing exactly what to believe. But then she had Daddy back. With a big sigh of relief she looked at Daddy, put her arm through his, and they left to take Mike home. Mike didn't even turn around to say good-bye.

And there I was, left without . . . without . . .

Orville stood there, pressed against the kitchen table as I came at him. "You miserable little—"

He rather set his jaw, the way Daddy does. "Okay, I deserve it. This time I really deserve it. Go ahead. Hit me."

He was ready for a major assaultive slap. He would take it on the jaw like a man. But he's such a cheese, he thought the better of it and turned, to take the blow on softer parts.

But what was the point? It wasn't really his fault. And when I was in the river drowning with fish, I could easily have gone down if it hadn't been for Garth, gone down without ever having said good-bye to Mom and Daddy and this little . . . this sweet brother of mine. I put my arms around him and kissed him.

He wiped the kiss off his cheek. "She's gone mad," he said.

Mad, yes.

I'd had the most exciting adventure of my life, hadn't I?

And I was closer than ever with Mike Sloane. I was going to be a detective. And I'd discovered a new dimension in myself: logic.

I opened the freezer and took out the rest of the mocha whipped cream cake we'd put away on the night Daddy had left, and I set to making us a really good dinner, what we all adored in our family: pizza from the freezer, a nice green salad, garlic bread with lots of butter.

I put the pizza into the oven to thaw it out. I put the mocha cake into the warming drawer to get the freeze out of it. I loved it half defrosted. Francine came bursting into the kitchen. "Okay, I want the real story! The whole story! With details! Come on, Ally!"

I set another plate at the table. "Are you still on complex carbohydrate or what? Pizza is pretty rich. You want me to fix you a big salad?"

She looked in at the frozen mocha cake, which was

beginning to glisten around the edges. She looked at the thick slices of sourdough bread that Orville was covering with garlic butter. "I've decided to be a writer," she said. "Writers can be eccentric. They don't have to be slaves to style."

I cut the vegetables for the salad. Mike would be home with his grandfather by now. In his room by now. Making his notes by now. Stopping and letting himself think of that final moment when he came so close, when . . .

Well, look at it this way. Mike and I were only in our junior year. There was still plenty of time. And we were joined together now, Ally and Mike, Mike and Ally, the best detective team Martindale had ever known.

And although I know that people like Margo Von Oster and sad Mr. Emerson don't happen often, well, knowing what I know of mankind now, being older and wiser, I was sure that there would be other crimes that would need a good detective team, a team that worked for honor and justice.

And the next time we finished a job, I'd make sure my brother wasn't around.

I ran my finger along the edge of the mocha cake. A little of the stuff was softening. I licked my finger. Ah, so sweet. Oh, yes, tomorrow was definitely another day.

About the Author

Born in New York, Blossom Elfman moved to California where she attended both UCLA and USC. She worked with children as a puppeteer before becoming a teacher of English and special education with the public schools.

An experienced author, Ms. Elfman has written several books for young adults including *THE RETURN OF THE WHISTLER, FIRST LOVE LIVES FOREVER,* and *THE HAUNTED HEART,* as well as a television special.

The mother of two sons, one a filmmaker and the other a composer and singer for a well-known musical group, Ms. Elfman currently resides in Los Angeles, where she is working on *TELL ME NO LIES,* another Mike and Ally mystery.

SCOTT O'DELL
A YOUNG ADULT
FAVORITE